Sarah Tucker is an award-winning travel journalist, broadcaster and author. A presenter for the BBC *Holiday* programme and travel writer for the *Guardian* newspaper and *The Times*, she is the author of *The Last Year of Being Single* and *The Last Year of Being Married*.

Find out more about Sarah at
www.mirabooks.co.uk/sarahtucker

Praise for Sarah Tucker

"gritty and emotional" *Heat*

"earthily honest" *Peterborough Evening Telegraph*

"a fab girlie read" *New Woman*

Also available by
Sarah Tucker

Fiction
THE LAST YEAR OF BEING SINGLE
THE LAST YEAR OF BEING MARRIED
THE PLAYGROUND MAFIA
THE BATTLE FOR BIG SCHOOL
SCHOOL'S OUT

Non-Fiction
HAVE BABY, WILL TRAVEL
HAVE TODDLER, WILL TRAVEL

Sarah Tucker

The Younger Man

MIRA

MIRA is a registered trademark of Harlequin Enterprises Limited, used under licence.

Published in Great Britain 2009
MIRA Books, Eton House, 18-24 Paradise Road,
Richmond, Surrey, TW9 1SR

© Sarah Tucker 2005

ISBN 978 0 7783 0264 3

58-0209

Printed in Great Britain
by Clays Ltd, St Ives plc

ACKNOWLEDGEMENTS

Big thank you to Sam, who is wonderful. I owe you so much. And Kathryn – thank you for looking after me in Toronto so beautifully. To my friends Caroline, Helen, Jo (to whom I sent a text in error and gave me an idea in this book – it can and does happen…); Kim, Linda, Nim, Amanda, Claire, Carron, Clare, Coline and Sarah, all of whom are extremely special to me. I am lucky to call you friends. To Will, who's given me so much support; I will be eternally grateful. And Jude, who's the best neighbour anyone could hope for. To Aimee and Mike, who have been angels in my life. To Julia and Nicola, for their support in the real world. And Dad, who's always there when I need you. Thank you. And to Jeremy.

And to the younger men who I think would probably prefer not to be named and who have in part inspired this story. Thank you for your energy, enthusiasm, sense of romance, humour and imagination. In some small way, I couldn't have done it without you.

To Tom, who is and will always be my sunshine and inspiration and the only true love of my life. I love you more each moment of each second of each day, Tom. And to Doreen and Hazel, who are my guardian angels in so many ways.

Chapter One
The Importance of Being a Sarah

'Ouch!'

Angie, forty-five, pretty in a hard sort of way, is taking care of business. She is, she unashamedly admits, the neatest bikini waxer in the world. I've been visiting Angie for years at my local gym. The GoForIt Fitness Club is an extortionately priced black-and-shiny-chrome ego centre for professionals, heavy on self-absorption, light on self-awareness. The purposely heavy-glassed building tries to be desperately welcoming with the Jane Packer flower arrangements at fifty quid a twig in reception, and the blinding white waffle towels in the changing rooms which everyone, whether they can afford to buy their own or not, nicks. The overly air-conditioned studios have lights that make members look far more blotchy and fat than they are—or as they are—I can't work out which. And the nursery is equipped with everything money can buy except carers who like children. Sit and listen in this place for ten minutes and you need not buy the Sunday papers. There are the wives and mistresses who twitter to acquaintances they need to know rather than want to know, believing friends are to be kept close, enemies kept closer. Their spindly manicured fingers swooping like swifts over tasteless, indigestible salads, furtively nibbling at the organic cucumber when no one is looking. There are the husbands who hide behind broadsheet papers or mumble into hands-free phones and window-shop at the aerobicized twenty- and thirty-somethings in their sweaty White Stuff gear. Then you have the tanned and toned tennis coaches in their whites, calf and thigh muscles deliciously defined, who strut like peacocks, their every word treated like a grain of worldly wisdom by emaciated Traceys who live in Barnes and Wimbledon Village who want to improve their stroke, on the court. The supersized eighty-degree heated swimming pools are full of noisy children watched neatly on the side by pained mothers who've just had their nails, toes, noses, eyes done and look ridiculous in the plastic blue bags they have to wear around their latest Manolos or Jimmy Choos. No working class here of course, but then that's not what GoForIt is all about. It's about professionals and professional accessories looking good and being watched. And it remains, despite the happy clappy attempts of the earnest club manager to squeeze soul into the place, as anaemic and false as the smiles on the ladies who Pilates through the pain. I go there for one reason only. I go there because of Angie.

Angie is sharp of chin and nose and wit. She has luxuriant long auburn hair and is permanently tanned, but genuinely so (no St. Tropez muck for her, she tells me) and is model thin. Long of leg, body and arm, she looks like a sexy spider, if there is such a thing. She's had two husbands, numerous lovers and several abortions. I think she has Mafia connections because she's always hinting at me should I ever want anyone 'seen' to, I should give her a call. I don't think she means waxing. She talks in a posh cockney accent so she sounds Australian most of the time. She's become my counsellor as well as my waxer. Over the years, she's seen me at my most vulnerable, emotionally as well as physically. And well, to be honest, as every time I see her I'm naked from the waist down, my legs splayed dangling in midair, like some gigantic dead fly, I feel it's a tad churlish not to open up lyrically as well as literally about baggage and stuff whilst she waxes away. She's waxed through my marriage (painful), the birth of my child (painful but worth it), and my divorce (very painful and thanks to focused solicitors Hughes Fowler and Symth very worth it), but her waxing always causes me glazed eye distress. It's okay pain. It's positive pain. It distracts from other pain, alternating between the exquisite pain induced by my career, the men, the lack of men, the sex and the frustrations—the latter two are invariably interrelated. She's given me pain. I've given her a few laughs. Luckily, she doesn't charge for the listening, nor the advice, just the waxing.

Today, she's giving me a 'target'. An arrow pointing abruptly upward toward my belly button. I'm here with best friend and soul mate Fran, who's in the next cubicle getting her finger and toenails French polished and eyelashes permed for, I've worked out, £1 a lash.

'Hazel, now put your hand on there. That's it. And stretch that bit. Yep. That bit. Yep. All in the stretch. And pull that bit over there. That bit, and hold on tight…'

Rip. The green-pea-coloured tea tree wax, which is allegedly less aggressive than the powder-pink sludge variety, tears fire into crotch. The green sludge is supposed to soothe away all possible pain. It still fucking hurts.

'Aghh, that hurts even more.' I whimper, surveying red blotches blossoming all over my nether regions. 'Are you sure the men won't think I've got herpes?'

'No, no, Hazel, this is quite normal. Quite normal. The blotches will disappear. Try not to sleep with any one tonight darling, or if you do, do it in the dark. But they might feel the bumps anyway and suspect something's up. Plus, don't have a bath, so they may not want to sleep with you anyway. Whatever, when the blotches are gone, you'll love it. You just wait. They'll love it. They'll get all excited when they see it.'

I'm trying really hard to visualise any of my recent boyfriends getting excited by my arrow. Their faces grinning inanely like five-year-old schoolboys who've discovered the delight of the latest PlayStation game for the first time. I can't. All I see are blotches. I imagine their faces contorted in astonishment and possible disgust as I seductively pull down the latest lacy almost-there pink number from Victoria's Secret to reveal one of my own.

Really? I thought most men like something there.

Well, there is something there. An arrow. And it looks sexy. If I were a man, I'd sleep with you, Hazel. And men don't like it messy. They're lazy. They like a challenge only if they think it's achievable. They don't like to forage for anything too long, Hazel.

Some men like a challenge.

You just wait.

Angie winks at me, as though she knows I'm about to be pounced on, tigerlike, by a prospective date as soon as I leave the room. I'm not convinced but say, 'Thank you, Angie. You're sweet.'

'So, what made you go all the way, love?' Angie asks, gently rubbing cream into my crotch while I try desperately not to get turned on. I'm not gay, but at moments like this, I wish men could stroke women more like women stroke women, if you know what I mean.

Not realising what she's referring to initially, I pause briefly and then realising she's referring to my decision to have a Brazilian wax, I answer.

'Oh, I wanted a tidy up. Something different. I'm the big Four-O this year, so I want to change a few things. Take a chance, I suppose, and I might as well start here,' I say, pointing to my crotch.

I look down at myself. My almost forty-year-old crotch. Not bad. Doesn't look its age considering what it's been through, but I don't know what an old woman's crotch looks like. Not the sort of thing you stare at in the changing room. Not the women's one anyway. I expect men compare size but women don't have that. I've occasionally asked boyfriends if women are 'different' down there. They've all said, they are. Shape, size and taste. Some hair is soft and downy, others, you could cut your chin on. Some taste, er, strong, others like strawberries. Yeah right. They've reassured me mine is lovely and soft and I taste wonderful, bless them. Not that I would believe any of it, of course. They would say anything to get good head.

'A fine place to start the new decade as any, I suppose. Must say, you don't look forty. You're in good nick. You don't have many grey hairs.'

'I have highlights.'

'I'm not talking about those on your head, Hazel.'

Oh, right.

'Plus, you don't have lines on your face.' (Looks more closely at my eyes) 'Well, not many anyway. Helps I suppose, you not being married.'

I smile. 'No, happily divorced. Must be five years now, Angie.'

'Yep, must be about five. Watched you go down two dress sizes, giving me a running commentary as it were. Spontaneously bursting into tears halfway through the facials. Angry one minute, sad the next, in mourning one day, full of excitement the day after. But now look at you. You're constant, well, as constant as I think you're ever going to be, Hazel, and you're happy. You're a right SARAH. Single and Rich And Happy.'

'I'm not rich. I'm comfortable. Happy? Yes, I'm happy

and happily single. When I had the energy to make space for a man, they couldn't handle a single mum with a young child. Now Sarah's all grown up and off to university soon, I don't know if I want someone else to care for.'

'They could care for you, Hazel.'

'No, it doesn't work that way, Angie. You end up caring for the man. They're all little boys—whatever their age. Frankly, I can only see the downsides to marriage these days. None of the upsides.'

Angie looks at me like a mother looking at her child whom she knows is fibbing. She knows me too well. She knows I'm a divorce lawyer and a very successful one at that. When it comes to talking to prospective clients about their relationships, I find a negative in every positive if I want to, and a positive in something negative. So perhaps I've started to believe my own bullshit over the years. She says my views are warped and harsh and cynical. I say they are realistic and based on observation and listening. A lot. But I have hope. And my colleagues tell me that hope I have, that single ingredient, makes me human. I think it just makes me weak.

'No boyfriends then?'

'No boyfriend, right. I don't have boyfriends anymore. I think when you're over thirty they become lovers. How can you call a forty- or fifty-something-year-old a *boy-friend*.'

Angie looks at me again, giving me a wry smile. She's penetrated my façade of ambivalence. The one I've become so good at nurturing and practicing over the years. She knows, Angie knows, I would like to meet someone, but it sounds so pathetic. That phrase 'Dear Agony Aunt, I want to meet someone.' As though I don't meet another human being in my daily life. Of course I meet men. I meet loads of eligible deeply unhappy men. They also happen to be deeply and overtly embittered and at that particular time of their life, usually openly misogynistic. And the wanting to meet people bit sounds strangely adolescent or alien or both. And it's taken up so much of my thinking time in past years. A waste of thinking space when there is so much more to do and think about and care about in this world—bigger issues, like, well, like world peace and the cure for cancer, than 'wanting to meet someone'. I'm thirty-nine, for Christ's sake. Not nineteen. Yet I want that singular selfish rush to the brain—and be honest with yourself, Hazel—to other parts of my body as well. That buzz of electricity when you're within three inches of the person's arm that I always misguidedly diagnose as love, and is the more short-lived but no less potent virus known as chemistry.

Angie laughs. 'Yep, men are boys, some behave like babies, like my first husband—I had to do absolutely everything for him. My second was more like a toddler, with his alternating tantrums and sulking when I didn't wear black suspenders and thigh-high boots on Friday nights. Most men are happy with fish on Fridays.'

She stops and smiles, realising what she's said.

'And my last boyfriend was in an eternal state of adolescence, angry with life and himself. At the moment I think I've struck lucky because I've got one who's about the emotional age of six—malleable, does as he's told, cute as a button and happy with his lot. But you're a youngster yourself, Hazel. Always think of you as a free spirit, I do.'

'I try to be. I've found focus and financial freedom in work I find challenging and enjoy and a happiness I couldn't have imagined in bringing up Sarah by myself.'

Sarah is my teenage daughter. She's seventeen, has lived with me all her life and is leaving for university in September to study French and politics and life. I will miss her. Correction. I am weeping inside at the thought of her going. But it will pass eventually. She added to my life in a way I couldn't have imagined. I felt I had one more person on this planet on my side when I gave birth to her. Whereas when I married I felt I dissolved as a person. I even lost my name. But perhaps it was just the man I chose. And what was true of him isn't of all men. I hope. As for Sarah, we've been a good team; I love her more than anything in the known and yet to be discovered universe. My teenage daughter, with her bright blue eyes and long shiny brown hair, in her Gap jeans and Quiksilver sweat shirt is grinning at me in my mind's eye. She's gorgeous and smart, but I'm biased. Thankfully, the A level board agree with me and they gave her grades good enough to get her into Bristol, where she says all the talent is and she can still have fun and get a fine degree. I will miss her. I will miss her dreadfully. Sometimes when

I think about it, and I try not to too much, I get a heartache and feel it's breaking. This sounds so dramatic but she's been so much a part of my life, has Sarah. I've read to her over a thousand times at night, and cherished each bedtime kiss and hug in the morning. Her favourite was always the book *Big Rabbit and Little Rabbit,* about how Big Rabbit loved Little Rabbit to the moon and back. I've nursed her through chicken pox and measles and stitches when her granddad was chasing her round the table and she hit her head on the corner and blood was everywhere. And I came and scooped her up and went to the car, running into the casualty department, asking, well, demanding someone see her immediately. And bless the National Health then, they did. I've had the pooey bottoms and holding-breath-banging-head-on-floor tantrums (a technique some of my grown-up clients also use in court when they don't get their own way), Teletubbies and Power Rangers (she always was a bit of a tomboy). I've met the boyfriends from hell and those from the local public school (usually the same). She's seen a lot of her dad and that's done her good and she's made her own mind up about him. She's meant I couldn't go out with the other adults on so many occasions I can't count, but I don't begrudge missing a single one of them. She's been wonderful company, both my right and left arm and I will miss her to the moon and back a zillion times over when she goes to college. And I mustn't think of that now, because if I do, I will cry.

A tear runs down my face, which I explain away to Angie as being something in my eye.

Angie sees through it.

'Sarah's off to university soon, isn't she?'

'Yep.'

'Miss her, won't you?'

'Yep.'

Another tear falls, so she changes the subject.

'So you think women want to grow up?'

'I don't know about all women, but I don't fear growing up. I quite relish it. I look forward to it. Hassles and all. After all, with age comes experience. Not necessarily increased wisdom, but experience. And I get more of a buzz, much more of a buzz, out of emotional experiences than I think many of the men I meet do, on all levels.'

Angie smiles again.

'You're in the minority then, darling. As for growing up or getting old as most people call it, I don't think most of the women who come to this gym look forward to it one little bit. I have at least fifty women in here a week talking to me about how they bemoan the latest line on their face, or vein in their leg, and how, if they had the money, they would have Botox, or surgery to lift and tuck something somewhere. Believe me, Hazel, these women want to hold back time just as any Peter Pan. Just as much as men do.'

'That's different, Angie. Yes, I agree, they want to hold back the physical aspects of ageing. We all do. I do. That wouldn't be natural, although ironically, that's what the ageing process is—natural. But I don't think women want to hold back the emotional aspects of ageing. Of gaining experience. I think they rather enjoy that bit. I just think they're emotionally, well, how can I put it, emotionally deeper, more interesting, more dimensional than men. They have the potential to have more fun with life if they only had the courage and believed in themselves a little more than they do. Like men do. I think women have the capacity to, well, how can I put it, to emotionally orgasm. Don't think men can.'

Angie laughs. 'Never heard it described that way, but think I know what you mean. So, let me get this right, you think men are rather emotionally frigid?'

'Yep. Well, the men I've met are. Both in my professional and personal life.'

'And simple?'

'Yep.'

'So if these men of yours are such simple creatures then, why can't you understand them?'

'I can. They're boring emotionally. We think they're straightforward because that sounds more hopeful, more positive, but actually they're just boring. Immature if you like, but they're less honest than children and don't say what they mean or mean what they say. Or know what they want or want what they need. Children are honest and do say what they want and need. I find men emotionally one-dimensional. Bit dull.'

'Not all of them surely. What about the romantic gestures they make? You've told me about some of the lovely weekends to Prague, New York and Milan you've been on care of these boring emotional insipid men of yours. They've been spontaneous with flowers and actions.'

'What about them?'

'That shows emotional depth.'

'No, it shows imagination. Consideration. Thoughtfulness. If they want something in return, it shows logic, probable manipulation, it doesn't show emotional depth.'

'How do you gain emotional depth, then? How do men gain emotional depth?'

'For me, was when I gave birth to Sarah. And when I got divorced. I gained an inner strength, an impetus, an edge, an understanding, a focus, an energy, a direction, through childbirth and divorce I didn't have before.'

'You didn't gain any of those things when you got married?'

'No. I became a part of something. I wasn't whole anymore.'

'Don't you lose yourself a bit when you become a mother, too?'

'I found being a mother is as whole as they come. And the mother figure as any religion or prophet or tarot card reader will tell you, is the strongest card in the deck. Most powerful. Most resourceful. Most compassionate.'

'So how did your divorce make you whole?'

'I got my name back and my self-esteem, having gone through the steepest learning curve I hope I'll ever experience. I rediscovered my identity.'

'Don't you think your ex did, as well?'

'He never lost his. Moreover, he went straight to some-one else, so didn't give himself time to discover who he was by himself anyway, which is why he'll never change.'

'You've been out with divorcees and fathers yourself. Didn't they have emotional depth? Didn't they show how much they loved their children? They've been through the same experiences you have, after all.'

'To be blunt, no. In my opinion—and from what I've observed—little changes for a new father. Or little in re-lation to the mother. Those I've dated view fatherhood as responsibility, one they are happy to take on, to talk about, to show off, but it's responsibility all the same.'

'That's a bit harsh, Hazel.'

'I know. It's harsh. I know. And it's disappointing to think like that, isn't it.? That men, the ones I've met at least, are that shallow. And isn't it so much nicer to be-lieve in the caring father figure and the romantic hero? The white knight. The Mr Darcy. Much nicer to think men think about their children in the same way women do, wouldn't it? That men think about women the same way women think about men. That they grieve and hurt in the same way women do. That they gain emotionally through experience. But they don't. Not the ones I've known anyway. They don't learn. They don't have the same nurturing chip as women have because, bottom line, they're the ones that need the nurturing. Even Peter Pan needed his Wendy.'

'So if you stopped nurturing them, do you think they'd grow up emotionally?'

'No. And that's the rub. That's why it's disappointing and futile to try. All of mine had this fixation to be and stay young, whatever their age, which makes them fun and fickle, but ultimately rather draining—taking from me emotionally rather than giving back. But I live in hope. I will never give up looking.'

I sit and scrutinise my crotch, which is now blotch free and quite sexy. I remember the time when I was in the car with an old boyfriend and he was stroking my inner thigh, gradually working his way up, and I realised I hadn't waxed for ages, and didn't want him to go there. I wonder what he'd think of this now. My cupid arrow. Angie jolts me out of my reverie.

'So, my love, how do you feel about turning forty?'

'Fabulous. My school friends are all turning this year as well. Meeting up with them in a few weeks for a celebration of sorts. I know it's not usual to say this but I'm quite excited about turning forty, Angie. Quite excited.'

'Good for you, darling. Good for you.'

I like Angie. Angie doesn't give me any homespun philosophies or advice, but does make me think. Thought for the day—are men emotionally shallow or is there a free-spirited, fun, funny, sexually imaginative Peter Pan out there who also happens to be emotionally mature? Please discuss.

We hug and smile and Angie tells me I have to come back in a month's time to have the arrow sharpened.

'You've got to keep it neat. You never know when you're gonna get lucky.'

Chapter Two
My Best Friend's Wedding

No tigers pounce on exiting Angie's little room, which sort of surprises me given her reassurance I would be eaten alive. I feel strangely liberated. Almost schoolgirl excited about the thought of seeing Fran and telling her (not showing her, we're not that close) about the arrow. Fran and I meet once a month at the Club, for herbal teas and sugar, gluten and fat-free flapjacks (they taste like solidified saccharined porridge, so sort of safe comfort food), and catch up on the latest gossip that's accumulated over the past thirty or so days.

Francesca or Fran as I call her, interior designer, also thirty-nine, one of my best friends, soon to be married for the first time to Daniel, series director for long-running critically-acclaimed excellent-rated series *Unreality TV on Trial,* whom I've arranged to meet in the café with her newly curled eyelashes.

I walk past the emaciated Traceys, the toned coaches, the spindly wives and mistresses, past floor-to-ceiling mirrors, surveying everyone in their reflection—not wanting to look directly at any of them, for fear I'll turn to stone. Or worse, become one of them. And I stop for a moment as I glimpse myself and think hey, I don't look bad. Angie was right, despite all that I've gone through with the marriage, divorce, psychotic ex, childbirth, childlike boyfriends and broken hearts, I don't look bad on it.

Fran, five-nine, curvy in all the right places, looks like Betty Boop. Her eyelashes have been overpermed. She's a good friend so I say, 'You look like Betty Boop.'

'Thanks for your support.'

'You should sue.'

'It'll calm down. Just that I have particularly long eyelashes so it's taken well, according to Jane.'

'Jane being the woman who's done this to you.'

'Yes. Anyway, how's your Brazilian?' she asks.

'It's quite sexy. She's given me an arrow. Which points up.'

Fran laughs. 'Sounds intriguing.'

'Yes, I'm hoping men will be intrigued.'

'You mean, turned on, excited, aching for you.'

'Yep, that's what I mean.'

Fran orders two peppermint teas and two bars of solidified porridge.

'How are the wedding plans going?' I ask, knowing full well everything is fine tuned.

Fran is getting married in a few months' time. She is organised. I know Fran is organised because I am her maid of honour and I know every minutiae to the politics of coordinating the reception, honeymoon, flowers, food, guest list and wedding present list. I know there will be no hymns, as no one sings them anyway. I've met the Keith Richards lookalike saxophonist who will play 'Blue Moon' while the register is being signed. I've met (and already slept with the lead singer of) the hip band who do excellent cover versions and will be performing after the speeches at the reception in the Abbey in Chalfont St Mary, where Fran and Daniel have their five-bedroom cottage, recently extended with cinema and games room. I have sat through every dress fitting of the bride (there have been six). I know the politics of which family doesn't like which family and therefore must not, under any circumstances, be sat next to one another for fear of distracting from the pleasure of the day. I know she doesn't like Arun lilies. I know her mother does and that last week this led to seventy-two hours of silence between bride and mother of the bride. Fran won. I know what she wants left out of the groom's and best man's wedding speeches and what she wants in. Daniel knows, too. She wrote the speeches.

'Are you happy with all the wedding preparations?' I ask, knowing full well she is.

'Yes, Hazel. Very happy. Think all my hard work is pay-ing off and it will be a very happy day. Only thing we can't guarantee is the weather and I've heard about this spiritual healer who is very good, and I'm going to see if I can get on her good side and ask if someone up there can do something about it. Never know, worth trying.'

Anyone else and they'd be joking. Fran is serious. I continue to drink my tea.

'Do you like your dress?' she asks.

'It's lovely, Fran. And I do appreciate you asking me to be your maid of honour, but, well, I still think, are you sure it isn't a bad omen having a divorce lawyer, and a divorced one at that, as your maid of honour. I'm not exactly an advocate for happy relationships, am I? In fact, quite the reverse.'

'Of course not, Hazel. You're my best friend. And, well, I've thought about these things, as you know I do, as you know I always do. And it's a good way to keep Daniel on his toes from the start, if you know what I mean. Anyway, how are you then? How's work, still seeing Dominic?'

Dominic was a barrister to whom I used to give a lot of work. Tall, dark, angularly handsome, recently divorced with three children, he was into hunting, shooting and fishing and was extremely athletic and competitive in the bedroom as well as out of it. I burnt more calories having sex with Dominic for thirty minutes than I did spinning for sixty minutes at GoForIt. And it cost me less. He was also quite sweet. That was until I discovered Dominic was bedding the female clients I was asking him to represent in court. I was miffed. As his pimp, I felt at least he should have given me some sort of commission. Anyway, Dominic and I were no longer an item—a team, in or out of the court or bedroom.

'No Fran, we're no longer together. It was a physical thing anyway. He was very good-looking, handsome, and I enjoyed his company. Fun and funny.'

Fran looks at me as if she's looking through me.

'He was seeing the clients wasn't he?'

I look at her and smile, but I'm a bit glassy eyed.

'Yes.'

Fran stares at me for a bit, then says, 'Hurt you, didn't he?'

I am not going to cry. I am not going to cry. I am not going to cry. I am a hard woman. A strong woman. A tough woman. It was a physical thing anyway. I understand what men are like. What makes them tick. It was just physical. Okay, I thought his children were lovely. And he was lovely when he was with them. And he was lovely with Sarah, too. I loved having breakfasts and lunches and suppers with him. And he was interesting and well read and I liked his taste in music. And he made me laugh. And I'm thinking, visualising him now. And things like this happen. I am not going to cry.

'Yes.'

A tear trickles down my face. God, so many tears in one morning. I must stop drinking so much water.

'Liked him, didn't you?'

'Yes, but, well, he had baggage. I do, too.'

'Perhaps. Depends how you package it, Hazel. How well you carry it. You carry yours well. Baggage only becomes a problem when you carry it around and offload it onto those around you. He sounded nice, but he had issues. You talked about him a lot, you know. Your relationship wasn't just physical. It wasn't to you anyway. What happened?'

I tell Fran about the clients. In a matter-of-fact way, without tears, embellishments or use of the B word.

She listens, sipping her tea, expressionless. She has a good poker face.

'Well, everything happens for a reason. You're worth more than him. Now hug.'

We hug. Like friends who've known each other for decades hug—without a hint of self-consciousness even in a public place like GoForIt. And a few more tears fall. Silent warm ones, onto her pink cashmere Paul Smith cardigan.

We finish the teas and bars and order two more teas.

'Apart from Dominic, anything or anyone else new or on the horizon?'

'There's a new partner who starts on Monday. Joe Ryan. Came from Wilhouse Smyth. Oxford, sharp, good reputation. And young.'

'How young?'

'Like ten years my junior young.'

'Handsome?'

'Can't really see in his mug shot. No one looks handsome in their mug shot though.'

'You do. Have you met him yet?'

'No, Monday morning, board meeting. 9:00 a.m. We're all being introduced. You know, usual informal, formal thing. We'll be working on a case together. The Bensons. Not particularly straightforward. Lots of emotion there. And money.'

'So no difference then really.'

'No. Joe Ryan comes well recommended.'

'Wonder if he's fit?'

'Business and pleasure don't mix, Fran. And I want to get away from dating lawyers and barristers. All we end up talking about is cases, past ones of course. It's a bit limiting. And takes the innocent romance out of the evening a bit.'

'I suppose it's an occupational hazard. You dated that banker last year.'

'Oh yes, him. The guy I met at someone's birthday party, invited me to lunch and then proceeded to tell me he has a girlfriend, a five-month-old baby and a very big sex drive and wasn't being satisfied. So would I be so kind as to relieve his tension.'

'Yes, think you told him to pay for a hooker.'

'In a nice way, yes, I think I did. Disturbing thing is, Fran, that this happened to me twice last year. I'd meet someone, talk to them, and they'd think that I'd be game for sex without the relationship bit.'

'Your problem, Hazel, and it's always been your problem, is that you're sexy.'

'A lot of women are sexy.'

'Yes, I know that. Let me finish. You're sexy and bright and come across as independent. You can look after yourself.'

'I do look after myself.'

'Yes, let me finish. So you're sexy and independent. Along comes a guy, unhappy with his sex life, but happy with the status quo of his relationship, meets you, thinks you won't get all emotional on him, because of the way you come across, and goes for it. Problem is, Hazel, you may do a tough woman's job, wear the blue suit, stand in court and be as cold as they come, but you're a big softy. And men may see you as ideal mistress fodder, but you're not a mistress. You're a wife, my darling. And they're very different animals. You're number one, not number two.'

'So what am I supposed to be, all submissive then? Play the little woman when I'm not the little woman.'

'No, be yourself. Always be yourself. Then you'll meet someone who'll like you for yourself. Because, Hazel, and don't take this the wrong way, you're not what you initially seem. You come across as feisty and confident and together, and you are. You are in many ways, but as your friend I've always felt when you're in a relationship, it brings out the softer side in you. By soft I don't mean vulnerable. You're not vulnerable like you were when you were married to David. You don't attract control freaks quite like you used to. But, and I know you'll hate me for saying this, because it goes totally against your "I don't need a man in my life anymore" philosophy, you're a romantic.'

'Perhaps.'

'No perhaps about it. When you're out of work clothes, you wear printed floaty skirts. Short ones. Your house is dramatic and contemporary, but it's feminine. Despite the cynical job you do every day, your glass is always half-full. And that's why you're fun to be around. And I'm afraid, an optimist against all the odds makes you a romantic.'

'An optimist perhaps. I don't see through rose-tinted glasses.'

'I know you don't. How can you, doing what you do for a living. I think you see more clearly now than you ever have before, that's why it's rather wonderful that you still have this faith. Just be yourself, Hazel. The right man will find this charming and find it, you, utterly irresistible. Mark my words.'

Two more teas arrive. We watch the high-powered aerobics class emerge from the 1 1/2 hour session of stretching, kicking, jumping. They look red and hot and smell of sweaty underwear. Most of them are smiling, high on the adrenaline and the knowledge they won't have to do it for another seven days. Neither Fran nor I feel guilty.

'And you never know, Hazel, you may meet someone at my wedding. That's where a lot of people meet their future husbands, so I'm told.'

'I do know. My next client met his future wife at one. Only he was married at the time. That's the problem.'

Chapter Three
Calming Mr Benson

Mr Francis Benson is screaming at me. Occasionally it pitches to a screech. Monday morning. Eight o'clock in the office. Mr Benson, my next client, is on the phone. As he pauses to draw breath, I interrupt.

'No, Mr Benson, you will not be able to get away with keeping all your money. You were married to your wife for seven years. This is not a long marriage, but it is also not a short one. It is somewhere in between and following the case of Jones vs Jones earlier this year, it is highly likely that you will have to hand over forty-five percent of your assets and a sizeable proportion of your income each month. Do you understand?'

Mr Benson, thirty-eight, equity trader, third marriage, two houses, one mistress, eight rented properties in London (none of which his wife knew about but will soon), one ulcer, does not understand. I sense he is about to spontaneously combust. He sounds as though he has been pacing, or is pacing. I expect he looks like Sarah when she first emerged from my body. All red and squished and in-credulous and cross-looking.

Benson spits bile.

'I hate the fucking bitch. The fucking witch. She did fuck all in the marriage. She had affairs, you know. One while we were engaged and another while we were mar-ried. I found out by reading her e-mails and text messages. The slut.'

I don't interrupt. As a woman and as a divorce lawyer I know there are always two stories to be told. People have affairs because they are unhappy. Because they are restless and bored and selfish. She may have been any one or all of these things. It's that simple. But I say nothing. It is not my place or my remit to speak. Mrs Benson's counsel will do that for her in court if it gets that far. I let Mr Ben-son vent his fury. Better out than in. Better here than in court.

'I sent her on loads of cookery courses and she couldn't cook a fucking thing. She brought fuck all to the mar-riage. Fucking bitch. Ugly fucking bitch. I fucking hate her. I don't want to give her a single fucking penny.'

I smile because all my male clients mention their wives' lack of culinary skills when they start to rant, as though they expect me to mention it in court.

'And please can I raise, m'lord, to your attention, the fact that Mrs Benson failed to cook spotted dick for my

client on the days he required. Failed consistently to prepare pasta in the correct way, with the right sauce. And
made, in the words of my client "a lousy cup of tea."

As though it's a big deal. It obviously is to them. The
way to a man's heart may not be through his stomach, but
it certainly miffs him if his wife doesn't cook. My male
clients consistently talk as if it's right up there with drug
problems and emotional cruelty. Suppose it is to them.

'Yes, I realise that, Mr Benson. Unfortunately, or for-
tunately I should say, you have two children from your
marriage, and you have to support these children and
your wife, whether your wife was a good cook or not.
She did, in the eyes of the law, support you, and you did,
according to my notes, make most of your income and
acquire most of your assets—in fact you acquired *all* of
your assets—during the seven-year marriage. So she has
supported you during this time as far as the law is concerned, and brought up your children and helped you to
become as successful as you are.'

'Fuck that fuck that fuck that. She has a fucking nanny
to take care of the kids. She fucking lunches and does her
fucking nails and gets her fucking bikini line waxed. She
does fuck all.'

I cross my legs at the mention of bikini wax, feeling
for some reason, guilty. As though a finger is pointing at
me. Perhaps it's just my arrow.

'Yes, Mr Benson, in the settlement her lawyers will
take that into account and probably expect you to continue to pay for the waxing and lunches as well. The way

the law stands you will have to maintain her standard of living or one similar to it. From what I see, her demands are reasonable.'

I can sense Benson is starting to pace again. I can hear him counting in two three out two three, in two three out two three, under his breath. He's trying to calm himself down, which is good and I wait until the rage has passed.

'Are you okay now, Mr Benson?'

'Yes, please continue.'

So I do. 'Think of the long-term goals, Mr Benson. Think of the good of your children. It is better you have as little acrimony in the divorce as possible because you will have to maintain contact with your ex-wife because of your children. I suggest you offer the matrimonial home, as your wife will more than likely have custody of the children. But you will probably be able to keep the house in Italy. This all depends on the scale of your financial assets, which I believe are considerable. Your wife is not asking for the Italian home and is in fact asking for much less than she is entitled to, Mr Benson. You do realise that, don't you?'

Benson is silent, although I can hear him muttering about 'bitch a penny,' and then speaks in a much calmer but no less emotional voice.

'Can I see the children when I want to?'

'The norm is every other weekend, perhaps one evening a week and two to three weeks' holiday during the year.'

'Is that all?'

'Yes, I'm afraid it is. If you are able to agree to terms out of court as far as access is concerned it will be best for everyone emotionally and financially. And it is good if the children can see as much of their father as possible.'

Benson is silent. I think he's quietly sobbing.

I don't like dealing with the child side of divorce. The financial I can do easy. Men tend to get emotional about the money mainly because they think it's all theirs and view it being taken away from them at a time when they want to burn their old relationship for the new. But it doesn't happen that way, as they find out, usually to the detriment of their psyches, not to mention their wallets. Divorces may be quicker these days, but they are no less painful. And the pace at which divorce takes place tends to only intensify the heat often exchanged between both parties rather than calm it. I've come to the conclusion over the years of practicing family law that given more time, I think both parties would think more clearly, with more compassion.

After a few moments I speak again.

'We could ask for joint custody, Mr Benson. Would you like that?'

'I can't ask for that. I can't look after them properly. I would need a live-in nanny, and no matter how much I hate the bitch, it's best that the children are with their mother. I know she loves them and no one will look after them like she will. So I will make sure they are okay.'

'Well, I think I have all your financial details and if you want to tell me anything else or feel you would like to ask for joint custody, just let me know. What are you doing for the rest of the day, Mr Benson?'

'Working, as I always do. Mind you, if I retire in a few years' time, then I might be able to get custody. All I need to do is prove she's an unfit mother. I'll watch every fucking step she takes.'

I feel a cold chill down the spine. Sometimes, only sometimes, I get a twinge of memory. Like a period pain, that pulls at my stomach suddenly and silently and disappears just as quickly. A smell, something someone says, a television programme will jog me back to a time I would prefer to forget. Like my own divorce. And I remember David using those same words. 'All I need to do is prove you're an unfit mother. I'll watch every fucking step you take.' At the time, it struck fear into me. The fear of not seeing Sarah grow up. Of being a terrible mother. And I watched my back. Quietly and consciously I watched my back. Now I hear that phrase so often from my male clients, with the same bile in their voices, that the only emotion it strikes in me is sadness because now I know when either party says this, they've lost the plot. And I've got to help Benson find it again, for his sake as much as his children's.

'If you need a counsellor to talk to, I know a very good one. I realise it's a very emotional time for you, Mr Benson, but if you can control your anger, you will benefit. As I've said, I know a very good one, and they can help in such matters.'

Silence, then, 'Thank you, Ms Chamberlayne.'

'Please call me Hazel.'

'Thank you, Hazel.'

'I will be working on your case with our new partner, Joe Ryan. He's very efficient, highly regarded, and I will be briefing him fully on your case this afternoon. He will be assisting me.'

'Does that mean my bills will double?'

'No. When he's working on the case, I won't be, and he's cheaper by the hour than I am.'

Mr Benson laughs. Which is good, although I think he's probably thinking along the lines of another woman who's costing him a lot of money.

'Good to know.'

'If you need anything else, please don't hesitate to call me.'

'At £300 an hour, Hazel, I may think twice about it.'

'I know, but it may save you more than that if you have some doubts.'

I put the phone down, my left ear still slightly stinging from Benson's screeching and stare out the window of Chamberlayne, Stapleton and Ryan. One of the top companies specialising in matrimonial law. I sit blue-suited, hair up in a loose ponytail in my small, white, slightly untidy office with shelves up to the ceiling on one wall, and a very large print by Nelson Mandela I bought at the Ideal Home Show a few years ago. The one with a lighthouse which I find very calming to look at and even chills clients like Mr Benson. My office looks out over Chancery

Lane, down to the street that is quietly buzzing with more blue-suited people, hurrying to their offices with trays of Caffé Nero coffees and bags of bagels for partners and barristers too lazy or superior to get their own. It's a sunny day, and it makes me smile…full frontal tears, hate and anger first thing on a Monday morning and I can still smile at the sunshine. Perhaps Fran is right. Perhaps I am a romantic after all.

Chapter Four
Meeting Joe Ryan

I'm blushing. I don't blush. Well, I do, but I haven't blushed since I was a teenager and I had my first kiss with sexy class lothario John Bullman in Mr Boniface's fourth year science class. He asked me if he could look at how I was cutting up my very stiff dead rat. I leaned back on my stool and he stole a kiss. I was so surprised I blushed then fell backwards, dead rat flying into the lap of Maxine Levine, who screamed the room down, in much the same tone as Benson did this morning.

I'm blushing because I've met Joe Ryan. I have that frisson of electricity running through my body. That double take. That slightly sick feeling. Joe Ryan has something about him. A presence. I don't know if I think he's gorgeous. Perhaps not obviously gorgeous in a George Clooney or Jude Law or Brad Pitt sort of way. More in a, well, a thinking woman's bit of crumpet. Like, well, like, I can't think of anyone at the moment. So perhaps I'm not that woman. I'm not a thinking woman because I can't think at the moment. But I think, I know, this man sitting in front of me, has 'it'. And I like it. Probably an arrogant bastard. No, don't judge him, Hazel. You haven't even taken in what he's wearing. What he smells like. How he's groomed. Don't judge. Poor man. He hasn't even opened his mouth yet. You've just walked through the boardroom door, briefly surveyed the room, looked down and he's sitting there. In fact, he's in the chair I usually sit in (bit miffed about this actually), light flooding in behind him like some halo. And he's looked up at me. He's looked up at me. He's looking up at me. And I'm blushing.

Brian Stapleton, forty-five, senior partner, good friend, Oxford educated, brilliant and unassuming, living in four-bedroom House and Gardens house on Richmond on The Hill, with his male partner, Orlando, is sitting on Joe's right. He is clearly amused by my reaction. I've known Brian for ten years, worked with him for five. He can usually double guess me—a useful skill in any personal relationship and absolutely necessary in our line of business when we frequently need to confer and agree nonverbally about clients in meetings without saying a word. He's ever so slightly bitchy, but that only comes out after a few gin and tonics at the local pub after work, but he's a loyal, caring friend, excellent, ruthless solicitor and very good cook. He's smiling knowingly at me, the bugger.

'Joe, this is Hazel Chamberlayne. She was on holiday I

believe when we first met, but she took me at my word that your credentials and attitude are impressive.'

He turns to me. 'Hazel, this is Joe Ryan.'

Joe Ryan smiles, stands and offers me his hand. My instinct is to lean down, suck his fingers very slowly not taking my eyes from his. I'm ovulating at the moment, I logic. That's why I feel so horny. And I watched Johnny Depp in *Pirates of the Caribbean* last night. But I didn't feel like this a minute ago when I was smiling at the sunshine. I must be professional. I must be composed and I must stop blushing.

'Hello, very nice to meet you.'

I give him a wide warm smile and stop breathing for a second.

'Very nice to meet you, too.'

We sit facing each other, and Brian starts. 'Well, Joe will be shadowing you on the Benson case, so he can see how we operate in the firm. If you could brief him this morning, Hazel, and put him up to speed that would be good. Joe's dealt with lots of cases like this before, so I don't think anything will be new to him but we operate in a specific way here, Joe, and you'll learn a lot from Hazel. Benson's behaving in a very formulaic way, as is his wife, who's hired a good firm of solicitors, so I don't think there will be any complications with this one. There's no issue over child custody, well, not yet anyway, and as far as I know, the demands on both sides are reasonable. But Benson does have a temper, and I believe Hazel has suggested he see a counsellor, just in case he makes an impromptu outburst in court.'

I say nothing. I realise I am still giving Joe Ryan the same wide warm smile I gave him as I entered the room. The smile has become fixed on my face and I feel about twelve. I'm turning forty this year. Hazel, will you please grow up and behave like a grown-up and not like some adolescent schoolgirl. This is silly. This is especially silly as I didn't want him to join the firm. I didn't want another partner to join the firm, which was fine as it was, but Brian wanted someone else. More people are getting divorced, he says, so we've got to have more people to service them. I was happy as it was and despite my attraction, I'm annoyed he's here at all. I don't want him here. And he's too good-looking. He'll sleep with the clients. Not good. I must have a word with Brian when Joe's out of the room.

Brian continues, still smiling wryly. 'Joe will be in the office next to you, Hazel. We're hiring a new PA this week, to replace Jennifer who's gone on maternity leave. As you will be sharing her as well, Hazel, I think you should both interview her, either separately or collectively, whichever you prefer.'

And that's another thing that's pissed me off. New partner but we have to share PAs. Ridiculous, but Brian also knows my thoughts on this and has obviously decided one is good for the two of us. So doubly pissed off.

I've managed to control the smile and the blushes and speak. 'That's fine.'

Brian then proceeds to discuss all other matters. Other cases in hand which I will be dealing with over the next few months, including one that involves flying to New York. Which is great, because I can stock up on my knicker drawer with Victoria's Secrets.

He talks about what Joe will be doing in the firm, and how we will work together. I'm listening and taking it in but it's all a bit surreal because I'm feeling some very strong mixed emotions—annoyed and attracted at the same time. And I don't find many men attractive these days. I'm not talking physically here—I just mean as people. Even those ones I meet out of court. I don't play the game of boosting their egos so eventually they can knock mine down. If they say they're not worthy of me, I let them. If they boast about their sexual prowess, I let them. And eventually they calm down, forget to impress or appear sensitive or macho and become themselves. So I haven't been attracted to many men. I've spent years bringing up Sarah and working and men have made an occasional guest appearance—usually about one in every two years, when I could fit them in. I would never introduce them to Sarah for the first few months, and then I would introduce them, see how they spoke to her and dealt with her questioning. I remember her asking Dominic once if he loved me. He said he did, and she said that was nice but that he wasn't good enough for me. One of the lesser embarrassing moments. The very few who I allowed into my diary and my heart, like I did with Dominic, they've broken it—so I don't want to go there again. And especially not with someone I work with. Fran's right. I do come across as much stronger than I am. I'm not as strong so I'm wary now, very wary of any sort of attraction—and especially one that starts in the office. Plus, I don't want this sort of complication here. This is my territory, where I am strong and confident and focused. I don't want a man messing up both my professional and personal life all in one go. But I've had the lightning bolt. I've never had a lightning-bolt moment. Fran is right about that, too, they do come when you least expect them. My heart jumps every time Joe Ryan utters a word. It's very disconcerting. It's as though I'm concentrating on the way he speaks rather than what he's saying. He has a dark honeyed voice. He speaks neither too fast nor too slow, with considered pauses and the right inflection at the right time. For fuck's sake, Hazel, you're analysing his speech. Hope he doesn't ask me anything. I've got to concentrate, but at least that gives me an opportunity to survey him further and take him in properly. He looks young. He looks older than twenty-nine but I'm sure he said twenty-nine. He looks midthirties, possibly early thirties. He looks younger than me. But not by much. He's got blue, no green, no (mustn't stare too much into his eyes now), brown eyes. Yes, brown eyes and long eyelashes. Why do men always have long eyelashes? I have to buy YSL extra-long eyelash mascara to get a decent length. Strong chin, olive skin. Or perhaps he's been on holiday recently, probably with the girlfriend. Or perhaps it could have been with the lads. To South America or China perhaps—or if he's square, Australia or the South of France. He's wearing a dark blue suit so nothing new there. It's well tailored and well fitting, but all men look good in suits. Brian always dresses well, but he's gay so that's to be expected. Perhaps Joe Ryan is, too. Probably for the best anyway if he is. I survey his hands. They are large and there's no wedding ring. Which is a good thing—although this may mean he is gay, or German (German men don't wear wedding rings), or perhaps he's just fussy and hasn't found the right girl yet—or has, but she won't marry him, silly girl. Or perhaps can't because she's married already. There's one signet ring perhaps given to him by his mother or lover or girlfriend. Or someone else's girlfriend. What does he smell like? I breathe in, trying to make sense of the scent. Is he wearing aftershave or is it his natural pheromones? Can't tell so will have to find that one out later. Over a drink at lunch perhaps. Is he slim? Can't tell as he's sitting down. Tall? Probably. He sits up quite straight, but perhaps he's got a long body and short, stodgy legs, his feet dangling off the floor like some five-year-old school boy. Perhaps I should drop a pen and find out if he's a munchkin. I drop a pen and look under the table. No, no, his feet are on the floor. Black shiny shoes. Churches. Euck. Churches, as worn by City Boys. Perhaps he's square. But Brian wouldn't have hired a square, nor someone gay, as he knows both wouldn't fit into the chemistry of the office. I pick up the pen and return to the table, Brian staring at me smiling as though he knows what I've been doing. He probably thinks I'm trying to check out the size of Joe's manhood. As if I could see. Not that it didn't pass my mind.

Back with the meeting, now happily convinced Joe Ryan is a decent height, well groomed, smells tolerable and could very well be straight and unmarried, I smile again, this time more businesslike (showing the teeth).

'I look forward to working with you, Joe. And welcome to the firm.'

'I look forward to working with you, too, Hazel. I'm sure we'll work well together.'

'Right, I think that's all for now,' Brian says, standing up slowly, indicating the meeting is now over, for him at least. 'First thing first, hire yourselves a new PA and, Joe, learn from Hazel—she can show you the ropes.'

As I stand to leave, Brian asks me to stay for a bit to sort out a few more items and asks Joe to settle himself into his office. Joe smiles and stands. He's about six-three I guess. Good height for a girl of five foot nine and a half—which I happen to be. Yes, have decided we would look good together, if we ever get it together. Not that we will of course. Not that I will allow myself to.

He shakes Brian's hand and then turns to shake mine. I'm doing very well. I think I'm doing very well. I give him a firm strong handshake, look into his deep brown eyes and smile naturally.

'I look forward to working with you.'

Joe smiles warmly, disconcertingly says nothing as though he hasn't heard me, or has read my body language and blushes and has already sussed me out completely, and leaves the room with one almost graceful movement.

I turn round and sit down. Brian is grinning at me from ear to ear.

'So you like him, then?'

'Well, yes, I'm sure he comes well recommended, Brian. I didn't see the need of having another partner, as you well know, but I'm sure he can help with the workload.'

'Got something about him, hasn't he? I think the female clients will like him. We're doing well on the male front because of you, Hazel, but we need more female clients and they prefer a man to represent them. I personally don't see why this is as female lawyers are invariably tougher than male ones.'

'That's rather sexist if I may say so, Brian, but you're probably right. I'm sure he'll go down well. I think he's a bit too good-looking. You know what some of these female clients are like. Vulnerable, and in walks this handsome man and hey presto, chemistry.'

'That's rather sexist of you if I may say so, Hazel. Joe is professional, will be professional and undoubtedly good for business. And as far as business is concerned sex has everything to do with it, as you well know. Half your clients fall in love with you when they meet you, and inevitably trust your judgement. It's all about building confidence and if they like you, well, it helps.'

'Yes, I know. He will be fine, I'm sure.' I try to sound as nonchalant as possible without sounding too blasé about Joe Ryan's appointment. But I know Brian reads me like a book. Thank goodness I'm not as transparent in court.

'I would rather my colleagues keep their relationship professional, Hazel, but if they can't I'm sure they will behave appropriately in the office.'

I look askance at Brian, who is still grinning like the Cheshire Cat.

'If by that you're suggesting I will try to seduce him you're very much mistaken. As you well know I'm wary and fussy and he's not my type.'

'Tall and handsome is not your type?'

'The office colleague. The younger man is not my type.'

'Good. I'm sure you'll be as professional as Joe will be. Anyway, we're here to work and make money, make more money and then make more money still.'

I smile and turn to leave. I know Brian could tell I like Joe. Joe could probably tell I like Joe thanks to my blushing, so I won't say anything but I do allow myself a wry smile and a, 'Quite. Well, if that's all, I'll go and start making more money.'

Chapter Five
Hiring an Ugly PA

We've interviewed four candidates who have to replace the irreplaceable Jennifer, who has left to have her second baby and will probably never return. She says she will, but she won't.

Last week she did leave, teary-eyed, arms full of flowers and baby gifts, waddling out the door to an awaiting taxi. Not only was Jennifer good at her job, she was good with me. She anticipated my needs and delivered before I could ask. She knew how to handle both her own PMT and mine. She knew when to speak, and more importantly when not to. I cried more than she did when she left. And now, I had to try to find another PA all over again, who would time manage my movements, but now, I have to share her with a man. I don't like that. Only-child syndrome, I know, but I don't like to share, especially PAs.

Especially with someone as, well, as charismatic as Joe Ryan. He may monopolise her. Perhaps we should get a male PA. Or better still he should get his own PA. But Joe Ryan doesn't want a male PA, he tells me. He tells me he wants someone pretty and young. I think he's joking.

So here I am, sitting in slightly messy office with Joe Ryan. We're arguing, no debating, well, debating very heatedly, who we should choose. They're all under thirty, two boys and two girls. All aesthetically appealing, all qualified up to their armpits and all hungry to work with us. We don't agree.

'A man. I would prefer a man. They'll be efficient and we won't have this baby problem again.'

I realise I'm arguing against my own sex here, but I don't want either of the two girls. Both of whom are very good-looking and very smart. And both of whom barely managed to hide the thunderbolt effect Joe Ryan seems to have on the female sex. Something he is obviously used to. So I don't want to hire them.

'That's being sexist against your own sex, Hazel. And Jennifer was superb. You said so yourself.'

'I know, but this is less likely to happen with a man. Plus, I think the two girls liked you.'

'I could use the same argument about the men.'

Yes, he could use the same argument about the men. Because I could sense they did, 'like me' (blushing, not able to hold eye contact with me but okay with Joe. When they were able to hold eye contact, pupils becoming dilated. Quite sweet really, plus annoyed shit out of Joe, so doubly good), but I'm sure, seeing me every day they'd get over the schoolboy crush. I will probably get over the silly thing I have with Joe. Not that it is anything. I just don't want it to get out of hand.

'Men will leave for other reasons. They will be ambitious, they will want to move on.'

'Well, how about we hire someone in their forties or fifties, a female, who won't be attracted to either of us and just be good at her job, happy with it, and has done the kids, marriage, divorce and remarriage thing.'

'Good idea. Why didn't I think of that?'

'You wanted someone younger. And younger isn't necessarily better.'

Perhaps the forty thing is getting to me. I've never felt anything resembling jealousy toward younger women. All I remember when I was younger was being more insecure, more self-conscious, self-aware, more self-critical and more blindly ambitious than I am now. I'm more settled, kinder to myself and with other people, but I smarted at the hint of him wanting someone young. It genuinely annoyed me. And I'm annoyed I'm annoyed.

Joe smiles at me. I know he's going to say something clever. Or something he thinks is clever.

'So we're decided. Ask the agency to find us a woman in her late forties, with the right qualifications…(and smiling) and preferably plain.'

I smile. 'But not too plain. We don't want her to scare the clients, Joe.'

Brief pause then.

'Brian tells me it's a big birthday for you this year.'

I'm taken back. That's too personal for this sort of professional relationship. I'm still annoyed he was hired in the first place. And annoyed with Brian that he's told Joe about my age. Wonder if Joe's asked about me, or Brian offered the information.

Quickly regaining composure I say, 'He did, did he? Yes, I'm forty this year.'

Joe looks shocked. 'God, I thought you were ten years younger.'

I look at him. Out-and-out flirting, that was. Can't detect signs of sycophancy or mock horror, but perhaps he's a good actor. Perhaps he's expecting me to say I'm as old as the person I sleep with. I don't. I ignore and continue the game.

'Combination of good diet, good lifestyle, good genes, exercise and enjoying my work, probably.'

'Whatever. You look more my age than yours. You look a good twenty-nine.'

So he is twenty-nine. He looks older than his years and certainly speaks with an authority of a man older than twenty-nine. He seems well travelled and has a wider perspective which makes his understanding of what is relative so much more interesting—and useful—especially in this job. I'm surprised. I must look surprised because he says, 'You're surprised. Yes, everyone thinks I'm older than I am. But it helps in business and dealing with clients—you know, the credibility factor.'

'Quite. So we've agreed on hiring an older PA, but not too physically challenged.'

'Yes.'

'Then I'll get on to it.'

I'm meeting Fran for lunch today, so perhaps I can pop into the employment agency on the way there. Four months to go till the wedding, and barring the thumb twiddling and last-minute doubts, everything's in place.

The Caffè Nero at the corner of Chancery Lane is crowded with suits. I think they're journalists in here today so there must be a big case on nearby. Two celebrities divorcing each other allegedly acrimoniously. I hear rumours from the two solicitors concerned it's not acrimonious at all, but the papers need to write something. And if it isn't, it soon will be.

I manage to zoom in on two stools by the window, sending a hack flying, and hold the seats hostage while Fran queues for tea and cake—getting two for us each in case we feel peckish and don't want to queue again.

'Everything is going very well, Hazel. I've tried to foresee all possible dilemmas, including friction within our respective families. Table plans have been worked out with political precision. All dietary requirements have been catered for. All invites have been responded to. All I now need is for the sun to shine on the day, and that would be nice. Not absolutely necessary, but nice.'

Fran looks contented and I'm pleased, very pleased for my friend. She's turning forty and getting married for the first time, and despite having heard some—although not the worst—of my client horror stories, she is 120% positive she's doing the right thing, to the right man at the right time. She doesn't want to live in sin. She doesn't want to have a child out of wedlock. Not because her parents wouldn't approve or Daniel's parents wouldn't approve, but because, well, she wants to get married. Not because of the dress, or ceremony, or friends being there, or being called Mrs Daniel Carlyle. Just because, well, she instinctively knows it's right.

'I know it's right, Hazel. Right time, right place, right man. I'm sure you hear that from your clients all the time. But I'm nearly forty, and I've learnt a lot, and think, hey, I've got experience and realism on my side and I haven't lost the romance.'

'How do you feel about turning forty?' I ask.

'Don't feel anything really. I know it's supposed to be the seminal year, but I've done so much in those decades, learnt a lot, loved a lot, and just feel this is a new chapter of the same book that I'm happy to be writing. So how's things going with you?'

I tell Fran about Joe. She doesn't interrupt.

He's worked in the offices for three weeks now. I've tried to find out about him, not the superficial him on his CV, the personal life him, without being too obvious. Don't think he has a partner because he doesn't seem to take or make any phone calls, but perhaps he uses his mobile all the time. And I'm not going to ask him directly. He wears a light but potent aftershave. Could be Eternity. Not sure. Don't know him that well yet, and hasn't got naturally into conversation. Not something that you'd just drop into one, you know, 'and by the way, what is that aftershave you're wearing, Joe?…'" He'd know immediately that I like him and I'm not giving him the gratification of thinking that. Our relationship is and should remain purely professional. Definitely. I've had lunch with him a few times, with and without clients. He likes vodka and tonics, champagne, teriyaki and authentic Italian restaurants. His taste in music is eclectic. He likes Led Zeppelin, Maroon 5, Pink Floyd, the Black Crowes and The Darkness, so obviously has some taste. He likes occasionally to eat with his fingers, which I quite like actually. I find it very sexy. I do it, too. He plays tennis, squash and badminton, and talks with knowledge and enthusiasm about the games, which reminds me a bit of my dad, who played all the sports till he was sixty. They're all individual sports, so perhaps he's not a team player. Perhaps he doesn't like sharing either. He's got two brothers. He's the middle. I like that. Middle brothers are always the most interesting. More challenging, more black-sheeplike. Eldest are invariably the most successful, most dull, most arrogant, emotionally immature and invariably unhappy for most of their lives (having been out with several eldest children and having married and divorced one, I recognise the trait). Younger brothers are spoilt and have their own chips to bear. Middle ones are fighters, manipulators, mavericks.

And Joe Ryan strikes me as a maverick. Out of court anyway. He's quite conventional with the clients, but there's something about Joe Ryan that I haven't quite got my finger on. And that's what's bugging me. Annoying me. Intriguing me. Okay, I admit it, exciting me. He doesn't flirt with me at all, but had mentioned I looked ten years younger than I am.

Fran smiles.

'You can draw breath now, Hazel. First and foremost, with regards to your age, you do look ten years younger. That wasn't false flattery. That was genuine reaction. I like the sound of him. He seems ambitious, interesting. Kind. And I like his name. Joe Ryan. Got a ring to it.'

'Hitler has a ring to it. So does Mussolini.'

'Do you fancy him?'

'He bothers and interests me. And there's that za za zoom. You know, breathlessness. Which is annoying because I'm in my work environment and it's not the right place to be feeling breathless. I need to be focused, not wet.'

Fran thinks the ugly PA idea is a good one, in light of my ambivalence (not) to Joe Ryan. I also tell her the CV details. The fact that he lives in Barnes, got a first in Law in Oxford and would like a Labrador, but it's impractical in London.

Fran sips her tea, absorbing everything I say by osmosis. She doesn't speak for a few sips and then says, 'So you don't think he has a girlfriend?'

'What do I care?'

'You care. Does he have a girlfriend?'

'Not to my knowledge.'

'Could work. I mean you could have a relationship.'

'Fran, don't be silly. It's wrong to mix business with pleasure, plus he's too young for me. And I told you, he bothers me just by being there. By being a partner. Plus, he's more suited to Sarah's age than mine.'

Fran is silent again, looking at my face and smiles. I feel like the teacher in *Village of the Damned* when the white-haired starey-eyed children were trying to read his mind and he kept thinking of a brick wall (had to be there— it was a good film). No I'm not thinking about sleeping with him. No I'm not thinking about sleeping with him. This seems to work.

'Well, agree with the business and pleasure. That's not a good idea if you can't separate the two. But if you're mature about it, fine. As for the age thing, I don't think that makes a difference. I've invariably found men and women get on better when they are from different generations. Every generation matures more quickly than the last. So older women and younger men are usually more compatible than men and women of the same age. If any are going to work, it should be this one.'

I think about what Fran says as I slowly make my way back to the office. Could I go out with a man ten years my junior? Could I show my turning-forty body to a turning-thirty male? It's not sagging. There are no stretch marks. It's well toned. Even lightly tanned. I'm also not afraid to make love with the lights on. But this is fanciful rubbish. Rubbish, rubbish, rubbish. He's a work colleague, ten years my junior, ever so slightly arrogant, driven and has that tunnel vision thing—albeit cute, and probably doesn't like me much anyway and views me more as someone who will help him on his career path or as a barrier, unless he gets me on side. Simple as that. Or perhaps that's how he operates. The cool and calculated seducer who uses his sexuality to get ahead. Just like many a female. Could or would he go out with someone with a teenage daughter who would probably think he was a bit of all right as well? What happens if Sarah fancied him? That's odd. That makes me feel very odd. My daughter and I vying for the same man. Oh, this is nonsense. My mind is going off at ridiculous tangents. You work with the guy—that's it. That's how you should keep it.

Don't go there, Hazel. Not worth it. Keep it professional. Keep it simple. Keep it cool. And keep looking for a suitable PA.

Chapter Six
The Friday Night In

It's Friday night and I'm sitting in my sitting room alone with my family size pack of Minstrels, glass of South African Chardonnay as recommended by Waitrose, watching *Pride and Prejudice* on TV. Sarah is out at the cinema watching something rated PG, with her school friends Hermione and Octavia (am I the only unpretentious mother at her school?). I'm trying to get lost in the romance of the story, but my instinct keeps telling me Darcy is nothing more than a poor girl's wet dream and Elizabeth Bennet would spend the rest of her life, post credits, rolling in domestic misery, undervalued, emotionally bullied and sexually repressed.

I'm cross. Perhaps it's because I'm in on a Friday night, my period is due, and the forty-minute run at 11.5 on the treadmill, one forty-five-minute spinning class and ten minutes on the cross trainer, hasn't managed to burn off the sexual frustration—which I think my irritability stems from. Perhaps. Or perhaps it stems from the fact my builder hasn't turned up to redo the floor in my sitting room. The fact the plumber hasn't turned up to fix the downstairs shower that spurts water over the rest of the room every time I turn it on. The fact my gardener, James Huxley, didn't smile at me as he usually does. Perhaps he's premenstrual, too. Or the fact Joe didn't come back from court today and we were going to go for a drink after work to chat about the new PA's workload (Marion Harper, fifty-five, married with three grown children and no visible signs of sexuality) and the hearing ran late and he couldn't and didn't get back in time. Of course, these are all men letting me down. And they're all things that I could do myself, but chose not to. Perhaps I should find a female builder and plumber and gardener who would be more reliable. I can't help but think to myself that men are simple, self-involved creatures. But then, who's being self-involved now? Here I am, feeling utterly indulgent, self-pitying and pathetic on a Friday night.

'Oh, Hazel. Not all men are shallow,' I can hear Fran whisper in my ear.

As I watch Elizabeth Bennet swoon at Darcy emerging from what looks like an ornamental lake, I know this is all bullshit. And I wonder how men and women manage to communicate at all. It's not that men think differently to women. It's that they think on different levels and at a different pace. Men don't care that they can't emote as deeply as women. It's not just that they can't feel as deeply as women, it's the fact they don't care that they can't. And that's the crux of the matter. Women think that the men care that they've got this emotional shortfall. Men don't, in my experience, give a fuck.

And I do. I do give a fuck, and fall in love, probably too easily. Three years ago, before Dominic, I fell in love with Harry, who owned a boat and a horse and a house in Vancouver, but also failed to tell me he had a wife in France and a mistress in New York amongst his possessions. Before that, I almost went out with Steve, but he insisted on seeing his ex-girlfriend on Saturday nights to celebrate that they'd been going out for two years. When I told him this was taking the piss, he said it was just bad timing the anniversary was a Saturday night and said that I was lucky to be with him because he could have fifteen other women if he wanted them. So I've had only a few men in my life since divorcing David. And of course, I've healed from that as well. Eventually. I suppose being a divorce lawyer didn't help my attitude toward him, anticipating he would be as manipulative and deceitful during the separation as he proved to be during the marriage, and seeing him match and occasionally exceed even my lowly expectations. Having Sarah meant it would take longer to get over the anger and sadness as we had to stay in touch and meet each other every other weekend for her sake. The being in touch was something neither of us wanted. And now, well, now Sarah was going to college and the contact wouldn't be as often or as necessary. Sarah could make her own way to his apartment in the Barbican where he kept his possessions—the BMW 3 series convertible (according to most of my male friends, wankers drive these cars, so am reassured by this), the state-of-the-art phone (as used by Uma Thurman in *Kill Bill 2*), TV (with a screen that moves where you do, er, why?) and hifi that makes a spaghetti junction out of most of his polished wood floor space. Plus a computer and PlayStation 2 and younger woman—ten years his junior, five foot nothing with dowry, primed to iron shirts and make pies and cakes, which I never wanted to.

Elizabeth is kissing Darcy, probably with tongues. Minstrels bag is empty and a bottle of Chardonnay has somehow disappeared. I'll text Fran and see if she's in.

MESSAGE SENT
How are you Fran? Are you doing anything? Fancy a chat? Hxx

Nothing back. Probably switched off, or with Daniel finalising the finite details of contingency plan C should contingency plan B fail.

Ten o'clock and I'm going to bed. I want to cry. No, no, I'm not going to cry. I'm going to put some music on and bop around the room. 'This Love' by Maroon 5. Yep. Have that one. I'm dancing slowly, then slowly undressing. Yep, slowly undressing. I don't need a man to satisfy myself after all. Some music, some wine, some Minstrels, the right mood and hey presto, I can do all the turning on. I dance over to the front door. Lock from the inside, just in case Sarah comes back early, before her mother does. Blinds drawn, curtains closed, lie on sofa and begin to stroke. First, very gently over my stomach and then up to my nipples and along the underside of my arm. Very slowly around my breasts, the left then the right, then down to my belly button and toward the arrow. The stroke becomes more urgent and I feel my back starting to arch and imagine my fingers are someone else's pushing deep inside me then out again, as I imagine someone else urging me to come.

BROOOOMMMMMMMM.

My mobile has received a message. The sound my phone makes when receiving a text message resembles a Formula One racing car just crossing the finishing line. Strangely appropriate I think for the present moment. I refuse to stop but the noise has taken the urgency away and I sit up semi-euphoric in a state of mild frustration, on the verge of coming but unable to. Expecting the message to be from Fran I read it.

MESSAGE RECEIVED
Sorry I couldn't meet tonight. Hope you had a good evening. Case went on too long. If you fancy a chat or drink later on call me. Joe.

I stare at the message. Friendly and to the point, text lacks intonation. I'm often having an argument with Fran about texting and e-mail for this very reason. Just because people can communicate doesn't mean they can communicate. And I don't know if he expects me to call him now later on, or later on this weekend, or if the suggestion to call him was meant or just a cursory suggestion, not meant to be taken seriously. But I'm feeling aroused because I've just been on the verge of coming and I'm reading the message and it's from Joe and the two events aren't mutually exclusive. So I call.

'Hello, Joe. It's Hazel.'

'Hello, Hazel. Sorry about this evening. The case went on longer than expected and you know Jonesy (Jonesy is Harvey Reginald Joines, cantankerous judge who should have been dead a long time ago), well, we were stuck there because of him, but you don't want to know this. Are you still game for a drink?'

'No. I'm a bit tired now. Have, er (thinking of what I've been doing), been chilling out.'

'No worries, just a thought. I'm staying in tonight as well.'

Silence. Perhaps he expects me to say something, or suggest he comes round, or that we go out. But I don't want to go out now. I'm happy by myself, and was very happy by myself until he rang. So although I still think Joe Ryan is intriguing, I want my Friday night to myself, with the pleasure of my own company. So I don't fill the silence with idle chat or suggestion. I let it lie.

'Well, perhaps next week one day after work.'

He sounds dejected but I don't care. I'm half aroused

and have had too much to drink and if he comes round now, may do something I will regret not just in the morning but the rest of my working career. I'm sure he doesn't fancy me and it's just my imagination so I might make a fool of myself. And I don't want to. So I'm practicing the safest sort of sex. Joe Ryan will just have to stay in by himself and mope or do whatever he's doing.

'I don't know. I'll see.'

He says 'bye' and puts the phone down before I can respond. Obviously, he's pissed off that I would rather stay in by myself or else he thinks I have a man here. Actually, I prefer him to think the latter, perhaps he'll consider this a challenge.

Now, right, where was I. Oh yes, on the sofa.

BROOOOMMMMMMMM. I must remember to turn that fucking mobile off. Who is this from?

MESSAGE RECEIVED
Sorry I disturbed you. Joe.

He's disturbing me again by apologising for disturbing me. This is silly. I ignore the message, turn off my phone and slowly, very slowly, make myself climax. Disconcerting thing is, I'm thinking about Joe at the time.

Chapter Seven
The Non-Kiss

Pied Paella is a little eatery just off Chancery Lane. It's five minutes from our office and serves aphrodisiac Spanish cooking (that's what it says on the menu) served by funky short-skirted, brown-eyed Spanish waitresses who wear black fishnets, black bras under see-through tight white blouses (two buttons done up only) and bloodred lipstick pouts. Lights are dimmed, smelly sweaty hams hang from the ceiling, air smells heavy with garlic, herbs, Rioja and lust. Joe suggests he and I meet there for a quick bite after work on Tuesday. He detects there's been a tension between us.

'There's been a tension between us, and I feel you would have preferred Brian hadn't hired me. I feel as though you feel I've stepped on your toes and this wasn't my intention, Hazel. Is this the case?'

That's how he put it immediately after the Monday morning meeting. Then he suggested we meet informally to get things out in the open. He talks to me as though we're opposing counsels in court.

Unfazed by his directness, I lie. 'No, it's just that this is a very small team, close-knit and when a new face comes in, it always takes time to adjust.'

I think it mildly inappropriate to come here, but they serve food quickly and it's not a romantic spot, which may have given off the wrong vibes about the meeting.

I feel a bit furtive leaving the office at six and not telling anyone I'm meeting Joe. Mind you, he's not telling anyone either, so perhaps he feels as furtive as I do, which is ridiculous, because we have nothing to feel furtive about. I don't think we actually like each other. Okay, he's physically attractive, I give him that, but he's right about the tension. I don't like having him in the office. He irritates me because he distracts me. So, yes, there is a tension.

We meet outside and walk down to the darkened entrance of the restaurant, greeted by waitresses and hams. We're led to a table in the middle of the room, so we obviously don't look as though we're about to canoodle (probably a good thing), and are sat down, given menus and told to order promptly as there's a large hen party due to arrive in an hour's time.

I order smoked salmon, wanting something light but with a decent amount of calories and fat so I don't pass away completely. He orders chicken in white wine, so obviously hungry or wants to make a meal out of the evening, which I don't.

He starts. 'So how can we improve things between us? Is there anything you or I can do differently in the office?'

'Well, I don't feel there is a problem. Or one that won't be resolved over time. There's always a learning curve at the beginning of things like this. I didn't see why Brian needed to hire another pair of hands, but we've discussed this and I'm fine with it. The fact I wasn't here when you were first interviewed miffed me a bit, but that's not your fault, that's between Brian and myself.'

'It's just that I feel you find me, well, irritating.'

'Sometimes I do. Think we may be from different backgrounds.'

'So tell me about yourself?'

I'm surprised he's asking me so directly. I start to go through my CV—school, university, marriage, law—and suggest he speak to Brian and some of my former employers. He smiles and says he wants to know about *me*. Not the professional me, the personal me, if that's not too personal.

'I want to know about you. If that's not too personal.'

He's wanting me to tell him personal things, almost as though we're on our first date. But we're not. We're work colleagues talking about work and life and how we can get on better in the office not out of it. I tell him about where I live. About Sarah and her aspirations to be prime minister or at least Wimbledon Tennis Champion in three years' time. I tell him about my little house of which I'm very proud, and where I was born, where I was educated, what my aspirations were and are. I tell him about David, and the marriage and divorce and how I draw on my own experience a lot when I need to feel compassion for the clients I find most odious. And how I have plans to buy a place in Italy, in La Marquee one day, and eat caprese and drink Chianti all day and have lots more babies. Only I'm forty this year, don't have a boyfriend so am pushing it a bit.

Through all this, he listens. Occasionally he nods, occasionally he laughs, and occasionally he says something that is just right, which shows he's listening and not staring into me blankly as he does sometimes in the office. After half an hour of Hazel Chamberlayne, Life and Times, I ask him about himself.

He tells me he is the middle of three children, born in India, having spent the first eight years of his life travelling the world with his parents—and loving every moment being with them and experiencing the world. At nine he was sent to boarding school in Scotland (hated it), then Oxford, and then into Law. His parents are both alive and living on Richmond Hill.

I want to ask him if he has a girlfriend but think it's too forward. Mind you, if I don't ask, he may think this suspicious, so perhaps I should just come out with it.

Drinks and food arrive. One hour later, we're on our second bottle of Chardonnay, and we shouldn't be because we have a case in the morning, and I need to be focused and it's only Tuesday and I'm already a little light-headed and finding the evening a bit weird because I still find Joe both annoying and exciting, and am annoyed that I find him exciting.

Another bottle of Chardonnay, feeling dazed now and ready for a party myself, the Hen Party arrives. He asks if I want to go somewhere else. No, this could be quite interesting, I say. About ten smiling shiny girls sashay into the room. They all look early twenties, twittering like birds as though they've been to a few wine bars before arriving here. The bride-to-be looks slightly dishevelled, dripping with (I presume) unused condoms and a large top hat with GETTING MARRIED on the front. She seems the least happy out of the group of girls, perhaps a bit overcome by the indignity of it all, or perhaps she's not sure she's doing the right thing. Or perhaps a bit of both.

Joe asks again if I want to leave to be somewhere quieter. I say fine, and that I've really got to go anyway and he smiles, pays the bill without me realising it and ushers me out the door. I'm tipsy, having eaten hardly anything and drunk probably two-thirds of a bottle of wine—rather good wine—but I don't drink a lot so it's gone to my head. And I don't find Joe Ryan quite so annoying any more. Or perhaps I'm just drunk. Anyway, this is all in a good cause. Hopefully it will ease the tension in our working relationship. He probably thinks I'm a cold fish and this will make him think that, hey, she can let her hair down after all.

He suggests we go dancing at the club Pisstake. An all-black nuclear bunker of a place that looks as if a submarine and space ship have been submerged into the heart of EC1. Grey suits and their mini-skirted assistants smooch and drink alcopops and Red Bulls and gaze at other grey suits and mini-skirted assistants smooching and gazing back at them. We stand out in blue, not that I ever thought I would stand out in blue—but we do here. My instinct says this is perhaps not a good idea. The atmosphere is heavy with sex rather than romance. But I think, what's the harm—knowing full well what the harm could be. But if I keep it short and it's all in the cause of improving work relations. I say, fine, but not for too long. It is Tuesday.

Maroon 5 is playing and it reminds me of what I was doing on Friday night, which makes me smile and aroused at the same time. We start to dance in the darkness, almost the only couple on the floor. Joe twists and turns and pulls me to him and away and I shimmy round him and giggle because it reminds me of school dances and trying desperately to keep pace with boys who knew their own rhythm but wouldn't or couldn't compromise it for a girl. Then suddenly the music slows and we're bumping and grinding and he's looking into my eyes and I'm looking into his eyes and our lips are getting closer but we don't kiss. And we're teasing each other and giggling and smiling. But hey, this is very sexy and lovely. I'm drunk but I know what I know. And we bump and grind for the record. I can't hear the words. I just feel the beat. The earthy heavy regular beat. And I realise he wants to kiss me but I pull back and smile and mouth *not here.*

After dancing for I don't know how long (I can't focus on my watch since I've drunk too much), I suggest we go to find a taxi. It's late and we have a case in the morning. He agrees and leads me, well, sort of carries me, up the stairs to the almost deserted street. So perhaps it's quite late. Must be after eleven.

We turn a corner into a small alleyway leading to a group of sushi bars and assorted restaurants. There's a tiny courtyard to the right and a small conservatory within the courtyard. I don't know if it's part of a house or part of a bar. It has plants and glass ceilings but it's quiet and he turns to me and he's going to kiss me. I know he's going to kiss me. He moves toward me and very gently pushes me against the wall, using his presence rather than his body to move me backwards. But it's not what I expect. He holds me, looking intense. Almost strained. He doesn't say anything. I feel, hold on one minute. This is a kiss. That's all. Nothing more than a kiss with a work colleague when you're a little bit worse the wear for drink. That's all. Don't make of this more than it is. But I don't say anything because this is strange and unexpected and I want to go with the flow.

I'm up against the wall now and again I think he's going to kiss me. But he doesn't. He pushes his face closer to mine and rubs cheeks. Brushing slowly and breathing down my neck, which I find odd and erotic at the same time. He holds my hair. Not pulling. Stroking. And moves his hand down over my cheeks to my lips. Kiss now then. No. Still no kiss. Shall I try to kiss him? Perhaps not. It looks so silly when I pucker up and it's not reciprocated. Feel like a fish. So wait. He'll kiss me soon. He still looks pained. He's breathing quite deeply now. Slowly, he's tilting my head back so I feel more vulnerable. And he breathes on my skin. And he breathes and he breathes. God, this is erotic. I want to shout, Joe, will you just fucking kiss me and get it over with. This is too heavy. This is too heavy. But I don't shout or speak because then he picks me up. He physically picks me up and my skirt lifts around my thighs. He pins me against the wall. And I sit there, in his arms being breathed on. I don't know whether I want to laugh or rip this man's clothes off. This is not a kiss. This is not the kiss I wanted. It's something else.

And then someone walks round the corner and he gently drops me so I'm standing almost touching him, and I stare at him, thinking what the fuck was that. Actually, I think I say, 'What the fuck was that?'

'Was what?'

'That non-kiss'

'I don't know. Sorry, Hazel. Sorry.'

His look of suffering is still there.

'I thought you were going to kiss me.'

He's silent for a moment. Then he says, 'I wanted to do a lot more than kiss you, Hazel. A lot more.'

I feel sick. Not, drunk-too-much-sick, more lust-sick.

As though if I don't get my fix of sex or even a kiss soon I'm going to pass out. Perhaps it was a good thing I didn't see him on Friday night considering the way I was feeling, but it's satisfying, deeply satisfying to know someone I find exciting, also finds me exciting. But I'm frustrated because I haven't got a kiss and to be blunt, I want one. So I say, 'I guessed that. All tense and frustrated now, wasn't an hour ago.'

'I know. So am I. So am I.'

We walk along the street, back toward Liverpool Street station, staring at passersby who seem as out of it as we are. Or perhaps they just seem that way to us. I'm energised and tired at the same time. I find a queue of cabs and ask one of the drivers to take me to Wimbledon Common. He says 'fine luv and 'op in,' which I do. Joe leans in after me, thanking me for a lovely evening.

'Thank you for a lovely evening, Hazel.'

I say nothing. I'm still fazed by the non-kiss. I'm not sure if he's teasing me, or unsettling me on purpose, or I've got it all wrong and he feels a similar sexual attraction to me as I do to him. Or he's playing with me, like some schoolboy. After all, he's younger than me, ten years younger—so I can't expect emotional maturity from someone like this. How can he start to understand me, not that I particularly want him to. We have nothing in common. Our friends would be vastly different ages, our social habits vastly different. We have one thing in common—we work together, and even that we don't do very well. All my reasoning and logic is telling me to leave it.

'You're lovely,' he says, nuzzling my nose, then moving away, breathing very softly on my cheek.

My mind is buzzing. Thinking one thing, then the next, then the next. It's one tangled mess of ideas and conclusions and possibilities and what-ifs. Perhaps this is all technique. All mind manipulation. Like remarking on a girl's jewellery so you can stroke their wrist or their neck for a chance to brush against an erogenous zone. Perhaps he thinks forty is the sexual prime of women, so he wants to try me out for size. Too crude, Hazel. Too crude. I don't really know what to say. It's not what I expected. I expected a drink and a chat, perhaps some mild flirting, but well, this was odd. Very odd. I still resent him. Resent him because I've just got used to a state of being by myself now that Sarah will be gone soon. But he's not what I thought he was. I thought him ambitious and cool and, of course, extremely handsome, but he became almost vulnerable this evening. Almost. I think I'm on a roller coaster, but it's dark, so don't know what's coming and whether it's going to be good or bad, tame or exciting. But my track record of reading signs is lousy, so what do I know? And do I really want this? Do I want to go on another relationship-ride again? They're fun but exhausting—rarely giving more than they take from you in my experience. But hey, what do I know? Besides, he'll forget it all tomorrow morning. And perhaps, so may I.

Chapter Eight
Meeting the Other Woman?

He's forgotten. I can tell he's forgotten. It's Wednesday morning and we're meeting with Brian to update him on our progress with several cases. Joe looks me straight in the eye, cool as a cucumber. Nothing. Nothing behind those eyes. Obviously, last night was meaningless. Ever so unprofessional of us both I think, but then I should know better. I'm forty, a woman of the world. He's twenty-nine, a boy. A mere boy. Thank God it didn't go any further. Forget it. He has, so should I.

So we sit, talking about optimising the client fee base over coffee and pain au chocolat and a mild hangover.

Coming out of Brian's office I head straight for mine. I'm vaguely aware of a woman waiting by Marion's desk. She's chatting to Marion animatedly, although Marion doesn't seem as though she's listening or interested. The woman looks up at me. She's about thirty-three, but could be younger or older. Can't really tell, but you never can these days. People don't look, dress or act their age any more. You get forty-year-olds clubbing and twenty-some-things vegging out in the library and chilling to Classics and Radio Four. She is tall, I would say about five-eight, with brown hair and dark eyes—can't work out if they're green or brown. Perhaps both. Wearing a pinkish dress with little flowers. Pretty. She has a wide face, wide smile and high cheekbones. She looks out of place in our clin-ically white office. Fresh-faced and almost rosy. Smiling at me, she introduces herself.

Fiona is Joe's girlfriend of twelve years. I learn this the morning after the night before. Fiona tells me direct.

'Hello, my name is Fiona. I'm Joe's girlfriend.'

Hello, my name is Hazel and I work with your boy-friend and last night I dirty danced with him, almost kissed him and seriously considered sleeping with him. And I think, although can't be sure, that he felt the same.

I say, 'Hello, I'm Hazel Chamberlayne. I work with Joe. Nice to meet you.'

Fiona Gilhoolhy walks toward me and shakes my hand. 'I've heard so much about you. Joe thinks you're amaz-ing. Don't you, Joe?'

Joe is standing nearby, with Brian. For half a minute his face looks like one of those TV ads which have now been banned because they unethically manipulate (surely all advertising does this) the viewers when hundreds of images are shown in two-second rapid succession. This happens on Joe's face. First a look of white shock, then horror, then realisation that he is looking horrified, then brain working overtime, then recognition that he should not look horrified, and definitely not look guilty, then recognition he should smile, then smiles, then recognition that smile does not look natural, then natural smile, then shoulders down, then composure. All in all, about ten different looks, all within 3 seconds. And I witness all of them. So does Fiona. So does Brian. Thank God he's better at acting ambivalence in the courtroom.

He turns to me and introduces Fiona.

'Hazel, this is Fiona, my girlfriend.'

I know, she's already introduced herself to me.

I turn to Fiona who is staring at Joe. Her eyes look a little sad now.

'I was just passing on the way to work and thought I would say hi and ask if you're free for lunch.'

Joe, now smiling naturally, appearing composed, as he would in any major courtroom in the country, says he is free. 'Yes, darling, although it will have to be a short one. About one okay?'

'Yes, that would be lovely.'

Fiona Gilhoolhy faces me, eyes still sad. Smiling, she says it's nice to meet me.

'It's very nice to meet you. I hope we meet again.' Fiona gives Joe a hug, one of those ones you give people that mean something. It's the sort of hug a mother gives her child, hugging tightly and gently stroking with the fingers, in an almost, there, there, motion. She closes her eyes. Joe looks stiff and uncomfortable. He's going through another round of more shock, horror, recognition, recovery and reciprocal affection. With meaning. With eyes open. Thank heavens I can't see my own face. I always was pretty transparent when I was younger, but I've learnt through personal and professional experience to present a mask which has become pretty Teflon-proof. Something Joe has yet to learn, me thinks.

Fiona turns and goes, briefly saying hello to Brian, who looks unashamedly bemused then charmed by her presence.

I ask Marion if she can come to my office in half an hour for some shorthand, then head straight to my office, saying nothing to either Brian or Joe, as my mind is now going faster than if I had had ten extra-strong black coffees. I close the door and ring Fran.

'Hi, Hazel, how are you?'

'Me, fine. Fine. Actually no, I'm not fine. You know Joe. Joe Ryan, guy I'm working with. Twenty-nine-year-old, sexy, you think there are possibilities.'

'Yes.'

'Well, last night, we went out drinking because he felt there was tension between us and we weren't getting on.'

'There is tension between you, but it's sexual tension, surely he knows that.'

'Oh, I don't know. Thought he did, and yes, I thought he felt the same, but he's twenty-nine, so perhaps he's not as smart, or emotionally smart as I thought. Anyway, as I

was saying, we went out, had something to eat, got a bit
tipsy.'

'Both of you.'

'Yes, both of us. And then went dancing. And then we
went outside.'

Silence.

More confused silence other end.

'And you kissed.'

'No.'

'You had sex?'

'No.'

'You talked.'

'No.'

'So let me get this right, you went outside, didn't kiss,
didn't have sex and didn't talk.'

'Well, he held me. He held me up against a wall and
breathed on me. Nearly kissed me. But didn't say a word.
He just looked into my eyes and almost kissed me and
breathed on me and pushed my head back so I could feel
it more and well, that was it.'

'What's he like this morning?'

'Well, he was ambivalent this morning. He didn't say
anything to me about last night and I thought, hey, these
things happen. Nothing happened—well, it did—but
nothing happened—and it was just one of those ma-
noeuvres to try to break the tension.'

'Despite the fact that it's probably added to it.'

'Exactly. It's just that I felt, well, that he was a game
player, that he didn't like me and was just trying to un-

nerve me. He was drunk and I was drunk, I should probably let it lie there.'

'I agree.'

'But that's not all…he has a girlfriend.'

'They always do, Hazel.'

'She came into the office today. Just now, this morning. Just popping in to ask him for lunch. She saw me and
introduced herself and said he had spoken a lot about me
and he looked shocked and guilty and lost his composure
and when she hugged him he looked as stiff as a board.'

'So, he obviously does remember last night then. Why
would he look guilty?'

'I know, I thought that. I thought that. But you know,
Fiona, the girlfriend, I think she's about my age, and she
looked, well, she looked nice. She looked really nice, and
sad. You know. Sad eyes like I used to have when I was
splitting up with David. She had those eyes. Rest of the
face, the demeanour was smiling. The eyes were sad.'

'Don't get involved, Hazel. Don't get involved. You
went out last night with someone you have a chemistry
with and you have to work with that person. You don't
like the fact he's there in the office, but you are attracted
to him sexually.'

'Well…'

'Well, nothing, you want him, darling, but you're not
going to do anything because your life is settled, you're
happy and you need someone in your life but not one you
work with ideally or with baggage. This guy works with
you and has baggage in the shape of sad-eyed Fiona. Not

your problem. Don't make it your problem. I have to go Hazel, meeting Daniel to talk about honeymoons. And by the way, don't forget we have lunch on Sunday with the girls at Le Pont.'

'I won't forget and thanks for the advice.'

'All advice is bad, and good advice is worse. I've just told you what you already know. Byee.'

Click.

Lunch on Sunday with the girls—Doreen, Carron, Valerie and Fran. All old school friends I've known since I was eleven. All forty this year. All different from me. And all of whom would probably tell me to steer clear of Joe.

Joe walks through my door without knocking, looking transparently uncool.

'So you know I have a girlfriend.'

He stands in my slightly untidy office at 9:00 a.m., in the doorway. He's wearing a smart, what looks like a Paul Smith suit, dripping with guilt and pheromones. I don't say anything. Why should I? We haven't done anything. Okay, we danced and we had this electric non-kiss moment, or whatever you call it, but it's not as if we had sex or anything. Then why am I miffed? Why can I feel something in my stomach go thud. And he obviously feels guilty. He feels he needs to explain so that it doesn't happen again—the dance and the non-kissing. I think about saying something trite like, 'that's fine', but I don't. I say nothing. This fazes him a bit. I can see it's confusing him. I can see he expects me to fill the embarrassed gap. I don't.

'I've been going out with Fiona for twelve years. I live with her.'

I smile and tell him I think she's lovely, which I genuinely do.

'She's lovely. Very beautiful.'

'She is,' he says. 'She is and I'm happy. And I love her. And she loves me… Okay, I'm not happy, I haven't been for some time, but we're treading water emotionally at the moment. Things are okay. But I don't feel for her the way I used to. I don't love her that way anymore.'

I freeze. I don't love her that way anymore. He said, I don't love her that way anymore. That's what David said to me all those years ago and that's what male clients say to me when they're petitioning or have been petitioned, usually when they've met someone else. And Joe doesn't love Fiona that way anymore. And hasn't done for years. And has been treading water emotionally and doing nothing about it until he meets another woman. And this time, I'm the other woman. I'm in the same play I was all those years ago, just a different character, with a slightly different plotline. Just like one of the those Elvis Presley movies which are set on a different beach, with different songs but that same scenario.

Joe sits down without asking and says, 'I've been thinking about you.'

He's been thinking about me. Thinking about me since last night or thinking about me since he started working for the company. I don't think it's the right time to ask him to be specific, although I want to know. So I hedge my bets and say, 'You mean since last night.'

'No, wish it was. No, since I first met you, Hazel. Since I first joined the company.'

I'm quietly very pleased, which may be just a pride thing. He obviously felt the electricity, too, but fought it like I did and that's what was causing, is causing the tension. He may not be married, but going out with someone, living with someone for twelve years is like a marriage. Is as good as being married. I don't know if they have children. Not right to ask now. And it doesn't matter anyway. This isn't going anywhere. So I say, 'The tension will pass. Fiona seems a lovely girl, and it's best to keep personal relationships out of the office. I'm not a relationship breaker—I've been the victim of one of those myself—although it wasn't a particularly happy marriage I was in at the time. But I don't want to get involved, so please don't tell me any more. As for the tension between us, it will pass. It will pass.'

He looks awkward.

'Yes, I thought so, too. I've been trying not to think about you, but I work with you and, well, it's difficult to get away from you. I've tried. Fiona knows something has changed since I joined the company. I just feel more distant from her. I feel I'm pulling away and she senses it. Thing is I can't promise you anything, but I wanted you to know the truth and how I feel about you. And I more than like you.'

What does that mean? More than like. More than like

sounds very childlike. Is lust more than like? Is More Than Like, Less than Love or in Love? Means nothing. Whatever it does mean, it's not right for the office and not enough for me.

But then I look at Joe and listen to him. I'm torn. I'm torn because I find Joe Ryan very attractive. Last night I found him funny and fun and sexy and sensitive and he makes me feel how I haven't felt for a long time. And I love the fact there's a mutual attraction. And minus girl-friend, or even girlfriend of under six months (which doesn't count and is within honeymoon period of rela-tionship so he should be smitten anyway), perhaps I would pursue him, perhaps like a predatory female that still thinks he is possible prey. But this is different. This situation is very different because it's me. And I can't, I won't do this to another woman. His relationship with Fiona is a long-term one. A long-term girlfriend, long-term live-in girlfriend of twelve years. And this hits me deeply. I'd known David that long when he met some-one else and left me. I was devastated and it broke my heart and I've never felt that sort of pain and never will be able to again because once you've been to hell you know what it would look like second time around. And not knowing is the worst thing of all. I don't want to do this to another woman, or help a man do this to another woman. I don't want to break another woman's heart. That's not fair.

'Thank you for that. And I don't expect anything from you. We were both a little drunk last night, and, well, I think it's probably for the best you try to make it work with Fiona.'

He looks surprised and then a little dejected.

'Thank you for understanding, Hazel.'

'That's okay, these things happen. We must ensure they don't again and we remain professional in the office and it doesn't have an impact on our working relationship.'

I hear myself say these words. This is all complete bollocks of course. Once sex is out there, you can't just ignore it or pour ointment on it. It's there and it won't go away. The more you resist it, the more powerful it gets. We both know that already. But perhaps I've nipped it in the bud early enough. Perhaps Joe and I have both nipped it in the bud. He smiles and goes and closes the door and I'm left alone with an incoming call from Benson buzzing on my phone, and another one from Fran.

I deal with Benson quickly. He wants to fight for custody which I tell him will be expensive and emotionally draining and if there is any way he and Mrs Benson can come to some sort of agreement out of court, this is best for them and the children. Brian would kill me for saying this as I'm throwing away tens of thousands of pounds in fees, but I don't want to make money this way. When it's to do with splitting money, that's one thing, children— completely another. He goes away muttering something about an unfit mother.

I speak to Fran who's in the travel agent with Daniel.

'Hazel, I just wanted to confirm you were okay with doing one of the readings. We want you to read the one about what love is. Do you think you can do that without gagging?'

'Of course I can. Don't be silly.'

'Good. Anyway, how are you? Dealt with the Joe situation?'

'Think so. I'm okay.' I tell Fran what I've just said to Joe. She listens and tells me I was right to back off. That if he wants to leave Fiona, he should do it of his own volition but that I must not, must not under any circumstances try to seduce him because it would compromise my work position as well as the relationship I have with him in the future.

'Hazel, men overlap in relationships, and so do a lot of women. You are single and available and grounded. Or relatively grounded. He isn't single and doesn't sound grounded. You have a full enough life anyway. Perhaps when Sarah goes to college, stuff may change but you don't need this. I've been out with guys who are either just leaving their girlfriends or wives and you get all their crap. Trust me, you don't want or need their guilt and angst. It's draining and boring and you won't get any thanks for it, from them, or from your friends who you will in turn have to load off onto. True, depending on how much you like him, how much you've allowed him to get under your skin already, you're going to want something more because you can't have it, and until he is free you can't have him. You have to deal with that. That is your issue, not his. But you know firsthand what it's like to lose someone you love, so remember that. If their relationship is not good, then Joe will have to deal with it, deal with his own guilt of thinking about another woman all the time—but that is his issue—don't make it yours. He will also want you more because he can't have you, but he will respect you for being decent, which you are being. So don't sleep with him, okay.'

I say, 'okay,' and say that I'm happy to read at the service and Fran tells me she loves me and is proud of me and that there will be a lot of talent at the reception, which I don't believe but it makes me feel better in a superficial sort of way.

I don't leave my office all morning, deal with piles of paperwork that makes my office look slightly less untidy. By lunch-time, I've almost forgotten everything to do with Joe.

And then, I don't know why, but think it's looking at the clock and seeing it's one already and that's when they are meant to be having lunch and then thinking of Fiona and I think of this morning and looking into her eyes. Her sad beautiful brown-green eyes. She knows. At that moment, I know Fiona knows or suspects that Joe likes me. That he likes me enough so that she has to be passing and has to make herself known to me. So that I can see her and feel guilty or threatened or sympathy or all three and that she can claim her territory and her man. But it doesn't work that way. I know as I've been there and I've had many clients through my door who've been there. True, I can walk away, which I have decided to do this morning, but she's got to work on Joe, not me. He's the one that owes her something—I owe her nothing. I don't want to feel pity, because that's negative. I just feel compassion because I think she's going to get hurt because his feelings have changed for her. If she loves him and is in love with him—which I can only guess she is, she'll get hurt very deeply and if she isn't, she won't. For her sake I hope it's the latter.

I don't see Joe again that day. I'm too busy with cases and backlogs and I'm due to go to New York next week on business, so I try to focus on work. And work only.

That evening, I'm in the house by myself again. Sarah is out on a field trip this week for geography somewhere in the West Country, and I'm nesting by the TV with Minstrels and some hypo health drink and a rerun of *The Office*.

My mobile rings. My phone says Joe Ryan's mobile is calling me. But I don't want to speak to him tonight. So I let it ring and click on to the answer machine.

It rings again five minutes later. Joe Ryan mobile again. Persistent, but perhaps it's to do with work. These things can wait. If he leaves a message I will listen. But not now.

Another few minutes, another call. Still Joe Ryan. According to my phone another message left.

Okay, I'll listen. First message. Sounds strong and almost businesslike.

'Sorry about today. I didn't expect Fiona and she wanted to meet you. I understand if you don't want to go out for supper, but would like to go out for a drink with you. During daylight. Less risky.'

Second message. Not as strong. Bit vulnerable sounding.

'Perhaps the drink is not such a good idea.'

Last message. Sounding tense. Almost desperate.

'I'm sorry about this, Hazel. I never meant this to happen. I love Fiona very much and don't want to hurt her. I know you understand. I have been thinking about you a lot, and I have been going through a difficult patch with Fiona, but, well, thank you for understanding. And thank you for last night. It was fun but, well, you know.' Click.

Right, well, that was it. One non-kiss, a bit of dirty dancing and I've known him for no more than a few weeks, just over. I've worked on several cases with him, so I know he's a good solicitor and wears sharp suits, but that's all I know about him and he's now calling me one evening at home and telling me that he's leaving his girl-friend of twelve years because he's met me. He doesn't say it in so many words but this is the gist of it. I'm the catalyst to him realising he can't stay in an unhappy relationship. But there's no guarantee I want to be with him or go out with him. Christ, don't know if I even want to sleep with him now.

But at least he knows he can't have one and the other, sandwiched between Fiona and Hazel—both of whom deep down know what is happening and won't be treated badly. If the women are mug enough to let him get away with it, I wouldn't blame him. But I won't allow it, and neither I feel will Fiona. So I go to bed thinking of Joe Ryan as in past tense—it was a nice non-fling, can handle this and fall asleep dreaming of Johnny Depps, rather than sheep. One Johnny Depp. Two Johnny Depps. Three Johnny Depps...

Next morning I see Joe and feel sick. I can't be pregnant because we haven't slept together. So unless it's the immaculate conception or they're now putting something in the Minstrels, I think I'm feeling lust. But I'm busy. I'm keeping busy with the Benson case because it's escalating into a slanging match. Both parties starting behaving more childlike than the children. Feeling vindication in every vindictiveness. So both sets of solicitors are trying to be focused on what is best for the children, which, at the moment, seems to be adoption.

Joe is still shadowing me on some work, but thankfully I am seeing less of him during the day. But as soon as we enter the same room, sit down, there's a tension that won't go away. Like two magnets, we're inevitably drawn together, though we sit at furthest corners of the table so that the attraction isn't too strong or recognisable in front of others.

I notice more about him. The way he laughs—a warm open laugh. His smile—easy and wide. His voice—quite soft for someone who has to stand up in court and be heard. He talks to me, of course. He occasionally mentions Fiona. I ask if everything is okay. He says fine. I sense it isn't but don't press as it's none of my business. It's not my stuff and I don't want to make it my stuff. I like the way he does business. The way he speaks to clients, being firm but unpatronising. I like the way he talks and listens to Marion, who is now smitten with JR, as she calls him. Does that make me Sue Ellen, I wonder? I like him. But I tell no one, except Fran, who tells me I'm doing the right thing. Behaving responsibly.

Chapter Nine
Lunch With the Girls

Sunday. Meeting the girls for lunch at Pont de la Tour. Large round table by the window in the corner. Crisp white tablecloth. Oversized wineglasses. The place has been our regular haunt for years. All mobiles must be switched off for the duration or they get thrown in the Thames. We're here ostensibly to party because we are all forty this year. Or to commiserate. And to decide what madness we want to do to celebrate four decades of living and breathing on the planet. I have a coterie of friends who are all unadulterated babes. Some of them have had children, some of them still behave like children, especially when we're all together. But none of us, to my knowledge have had any nips or tucks or Botox and we've all worked very hard at life to look this good and be this lucky.

There's Fran, the soon to be married. Carron, the soon to be divorced. Valerie, the soon to be mother. Doreen, the soon to be CEO of one of the largest multinationals in the country. And me, who's been married, divorced, given birth, made partner in law firm and is soon to be getting laid. I hope by a man ten years my junior who somehow manages to excite me just by knowing he exists. We all went to the same infant and junior school. We are all totally different, and to my knowledge, we all love each other and talk with a candour about everything that would make most men blush. And does, when they have an adjacent table to us at any restaurant where we deign to have our meetings. We haven't seen each other for four months. I've seen Francesca more because I'm her maid of honour, but the others have all been travelling or away or doing something.

Doreen is late. She's always late but we forgive her because she has a huge budget and works in a highly testosteroned office of men in their forties who are deeply in awe of her and want to fuck her. She tells us so herself. She works on a Sunday so that she's two steps ahead of everyone else on Monday morning. Married to Mick the Big Dick (due to the size of his ego) with three hot-housed children all at St Paul's. She's worked hard for the seat on the board. Got the Chair through sheer hard work and hasn't slept her way to the top. She is loaded. As in financially, as in her own right. She's been studying martial arts so she can, as she puts it, 'slice the fucking head off anyone who suggests I've sucked or fucked my way to the top.' Quite. Five foot nine, size ten, Gucci, likes using word fuck, visits personal trainer three times a week (exercise and sex), cheekbones to slice a diamond with. Lived many lives in one lifetime already. Doreen kicks arse—ours and her own.

Carron, former MD of advertising company and soon to be divorced from dick brain Dennis. She is at the stage where she is tragic and numb and very wired and doesn't know really where she is and what she's doing. She's at the phone-friends-at-three-o'clock-and-four-o'clock-and-five-o'clock-in-the-morning stage. She thinks she still loves her husband. We're here to help her when she has the bottom-of-the-stair-sobbing-at-midnight moments and tell her that he didn't and doesn't deserve her and should eat shit and die. And that he probably still loves her but thinks he doesn't (This is complete bollocks. Dennis was and is a unmitigating prat who shouldn't be drawing breath, and only wishes Carron to live long so he can continue to bully her emotionally). The man told her so himself. Size six and reducing, five foot five, having daily massages at the moment, buys at MK Maxx, and counselling three times a week. Don't mention Charlotte—the name of other woman. Carron has kissed arse for far too long.

Valerie, former headmistress, is eight months pregnant and having had five IVF treatments is finally giving birth to a little boy who hasn't got a clue how precious he is or how he will be absolutely adored and besotted with, when he is born. I am sure Valerie will become the Mother Superior on giving birth. I feel sort of sorry for this little baby already. Valerie doesn't leave home without her tarot cards and believes in star signs to the extent she's timed the birth so she has an Arien Wood Dragon. Whatever the hell that is. She comes from a very close family. Well, by close I mean, they don't tell each other anything important, but they interfere a lot in her life and that of her husband. This is okay, because his family also interferes a lot in their life, so it sort of balances it out. She has decided she's waited so long for the baby that she mustn't do anything. That includes lifting plates, shopping, cooking and walking. It's a miracle she's turned up to this. Harry, her very understanding husband (she says he is, and I hope so) does everything. As are the parents and in-laws who are coming round every day to see how she is, and piss off the midwife. Size, fuck knows, getting on size twenty probably, buys at Mothercare, goes to toilet fifty times a day. Don't mention sexual urges. As for her backside, she's a Teletubby.

Fran, interior designer, fully qualified and profit earning, not just evening classed and playing at it, is happy with life as she knows it. Excited about the forthcoming nuptials to Daniel (kind but wet, and not in the trickle down the leg sort of way) and getting married before she's forty. Wanted initially small affair in Tuscany, now decided on huge invite in poshest bit of Surrey. Romantic, shrewd. My favourite. Size eight, buys La Perla, Peter Jones wedding list three times a day, don't mention divorce (must remember to not sit her next to Carron). Does her bum look big in this? (Yes, but only because her waist is so tiny.)

And me. Divorce lawyer. Partner. Divorced of course (how can you sell the product if you haven't experienced it yourself). With seventeen-year-old daughter Sarah, ten goldfish and two tortoises running wild, living in sought-after (according to local estate agents who sold it to me for extortionate price) three bed Victorian villa in Wimble-don. On speaking terms with ex (David and I say hello and make brief eye contact when Sarah is picked up/dropped off every other weekend). According to astrological chart, I am ambitious, kind, lucky, impatient and unprejudiced. According to mirror—I have no cellulite, some grey hairs. Can do box splits after long workout, ski on blues and surf really small waves. Size eight but only in posh clothes and when not time of the month. Interesting but not irrespon-sible sex life since divorce. *Marie Claire* magazine once pro-filed me as a Smug single with good prospects. Yeah right.

We haven't all been together like this for ages, so we will discuss everything from religion, politics and sex, to childbirth (obviously given one of us is having a baby im-minently, possibly at the table by the look of Valerie. SHE IS HUGE), divorce (Carron looks as though she's going to explode but for different reasons), marriage (Fran has a lot to tell about the wedding and will, but hopefully in precis form), death (okay, we're forty this year but we've at least hopefully got another thirty to go) and men (the understanding of them and having sex with). Not nec-essarily in that order.

Doreen starts the proceedings.

'So how is everyone? Who wants to start? And how long has everyone got for lunch?'

My friend, dear as she is, has an irritating habit of turning our lunches initially into meetings. She has an over-developed time management chip which is usually useful but occasionally annoying. She takes an hour to chill. She chairs so much in her job, that it filters over into her private life. She drives Mick nuts, but I think he's as officious as she is. We still love her of course, as we've known her for over thirty years and saw her develop into this withering career woman. But we all know, deep down, she's a teddy bear.

All the girls say they've got to get back to someone or for something by three.

'No, no one to get back to,' Carron answers, eyes glazed and red.

'Better than going home to Dennis. He was always chasing you up about who you were with, how long you were going to be. You've got your freedom. Use it,' says Doreen. 'Use the scorch and burn approach to ending relationships. Men do.'

Then Doreen turns to me. 'Hazel? You got to get back early? A man or anything?'

For some reason, Doreen thinks as I am single, I am having endless gratuitous sex every night. That as I am single, and Sarah doesn't need babysitting, I can go off with carefree abandon for long weekends to Bath and Le Manoir aux Quat'saisons (two of my favourite places for long weekends), and am on some sort of superwoman fuckfest to undo all the celibacy I had to endure when married to David (he said he didn't trust or respect me so couldn't sleep with me but that is another story).

'Actually, there is someone. Someone I like, but he's not waiting home for me with slippers and a condom,' I say, fiddling with the flower decoration which I find rather pretentious so I'm quite enjoying slowly destroying it. 'But I've got some work to catch up on. I've got a good three hours to listen and tell all.'

'Oh, tell us about him.' Valerie beams. 'I need some light relief. I've been having the most awful back pain. I've put on three stone, you know.'

The girls smile. Valerie says this as though we haven't noticed. She is huge. As in Sumo wrestler huge. As in puffer fish at full blow in *Finding Nemo* huge.

'It's just water retention,' Valerie explains.

I can feel Doreen aching to say 'This is complete bollocks,' but she doesn't. Of course, it's not water retention. It's the fact Valerie hasn't stopped eating and has done nothing apart from breathe since she discovered she was pregnant. She looks like two people rolled into one and requires two seats rather than one at a restaurant that typically entertains anorexic ambitious neurotic moody secretaries being dined by control freak public school anally inclined bosses.

'The guy is a work colleague and—'

Doreen interrupts, 'Never fucking works. Don't go there. Don't fuck him. You haven't fucked him, have you, darling?'

'I am fully aware of the pitfalls of having a relation-ship at work.'

'You've fucked him, haven't you?'

'I haven't. We haven't even kissed.' I don't want to ex-plain to her my non-kiss was actually more intense, more exciting, more erotic than a kiss would ever have been. So I go into work spiel.

'I know what happens as I deal with a lot of the di-vorces which occur as a result of affairs in the workplace. And we've got to cross that bridge when we come to it. At the moment, it's fine. If it becomes a problem, we will deal with it.'

'So you've slept with him. Not just a fuck?'

Shall I just make something up and say, yes, I've slept with him and then Doreen will drop this? Mind you, then she'll just ask what he was like, how big, how wide, how long did it go on for, any party or kinky tricks, where I met him, does he have a friend, so perhaps not. I'm not that good a storyteller. So I say, 'We haven't slept with each other, but, he may have relationship potential. He's fun and sexy and, well, he excites me.'

Doreen looks bemused.

'And you haven't slept with him?'

'No.'

'And he excites you?'

'Yes.'

'Mentally as well as physically—well, you don't know about the physical so he could be crap in bed, but the mental excites you?'

'Yes.'

She smiles. 'He excites you and you find him sexy and he's been working with you for how many months.'

'A couple.'

'And you haven't slept with him? Mmm. Does he have a girlfriend?'

'Yes, living with her for twelve years.'

Sharp intake of breath from friends of the round table. Everyone avoids Carron's eyeline.

'How old?'

'Twenty-nine.'

'A baby. Well, that's that then. Long-term, live-in girl-friend, good as married, younger man, work colleague. You pick 'em. Can't you pick an old barrister with a grown-up family and house in the country, or some-thing? Something simple.'

'I did. He was two-timing me.'

'So this seems easier, does it?'

'No. That's why I'm not pursuing it, but there's chem-istry and I'm being professional.'

'So you don't want to sleep with him?'

'No.'

'Liar.'

'I've been through the heartache myself, Doreen. I'm not going to inflict it on another woman. It's his stuff to deal with not mine.'

'What's he like?' Valerie asks eagerly.

'Handsome, dashing some might say, bright, sexy—and young.'

Carron says quietly, 'People seem to go for the younger flesh these days, don't they?'

Carron's bottom lip trembles. Waiter, Angus, comes over with the menus and asks us what we would like to drink, which dispels the moment. Lip stops trembling.

Angus is the best waiter in London. There may be better; I haven't been to all the restaurants, so in my experience I would say he's the best. I have known Angus for over ten years. He's seen me in the same state as Carron—post-divorce stress—so recognises the tell-tale signs of endless tears and dramatic loss of weight. He's forty-five, gay and immaculately groomed, extremely indiscreet with gossip, but only if it's of a kinky and deeply sexual nature and he's never malicious. Doreen has vodka martini, shaken and stirred, Valerie and Carron just water and Fran orders a glass of the South African Chardonnay she's ordered for her wedding and happens to be on Le Pont's extensive wine list. I order a kir royale.

Angus smiles and begins, 'Specials today are halibut and monkfish. I recommend the halibut. Very good, very light and—'

Doreen interrupts. 'Very expensive by the look of it.'

Angus stares at Doreen blankly. 'Yes, very expensive. But if you would like a child's portion, that will be half the price but all the flavour and—'

Doreen interrupts again. 'No. I'll have a whole fish, thank you.'

'Can you give us five more minutes to decide?' asks Fran.

'Certainly.' Angus nods.

'No, no, we can decide now,' says Doreen.

'Doreen! Don't be so bossy. Angus, can you give us five minutes while we sit on our friend,' says Fran, being wonderfully assertive and putting Doreen in a position she rarely goes to in or out of the bedroom or boardroom. Submissive.

Angus smiles again, this time for real. He turns and goes.

I snap. 'What is your problem, Doreen? You're as tight as a top at the moment.'

'Oh, work, and stuff. Home stuff. And I think Mick's having an affair,' she replies.

At which point Carron bursts into tears. This is good. The fact that she sobs for a good ten minutes becomes a bit worrying, as well as exhausting, for her to do and for us to watch. But as I've been there myself and have seen many women and a few men in the same situation, I know what to say, what not to say, how to say it and when to say it. It's affecting me more than it does with clients who spend £300 excluding tax in my office sobbing uncontrollably for hours on end because Carron is a friend and I not only feel her pain, I want to take it on. I'm also not charging for the tears or the advice. I don't want her to have the full burden. I don't want her to handle the pain alone. But I can't offload the pain that way. Experience has taught me I can't.

So as I'm sitting next to her, I lean over and hug her for the full duration. My blouse is soaked with her tears by the time she eventually raises her heavy head. I can tell she can't physically get up out of the chair because she's distraught with grief so I just hug her like I used to do Sarah when she was seven and had just returned from school, crying because some eight-year-old had punched her in the face. I was never a conventional mother. I told Sarah next time the eight-year-old punched her, she should punch her back and continue to punch her back really hard until she was on the ground, and say to her she would get the same treatment if she ever did it again. I remember telling her to have as many of her friends around her when it happened as possible so they could act as witnesses to the bully's defeat. It worked. Of course, I was called in and Sarah was accused of being troublesome in the playground and I met the aforementioned eight-year-old's mother, a coward and a bully herself. I told her and the teacher that it was very much up to the children to deal with life in the playground because it was just the same in the outside world, just that the playground was bigger and the guns and swords and knives were real and that words do hurt and are able to injure and kill. But that the arguments were just as petty and usually about possession and jealousy and greed. She didn't really have an answer for that. But Sarah never got hit by the eight-year-old again and nor did anyone else in that particular playground by that particular bully.

Carron's a noisy crier, and I identify with that. When I'm that distressed, quite frankly, I don't give a damn who hears me. I just cry. None of the girls say anything. They just sit and look on sympathetically. And Valerie gets watery-eyed and Fran feels a tinge of discomfort because she's just getting married in a few months and I can sense is getting pangs about am I doing the right thing if it causes so much pain if it goes wrong. Hell, I would be if I were her.

Even Angus realises he should wait till the sobbing subsides before he returns with the drinks.

She gradually quietens and just hugs me. Angus distributes the drinks and says he'll return in five for orders for the food.

Even Doreen just smiles and nods.

Carron lifts her head and looks at me and says 'So sorry, Hazel. I've got mascara all over your blouse. And it's soaking wet.'

'It doesn't matter, Carron.'

She turns round to all the others. 'I'm so sorry, chaps.'

Valerie tries to lean over to hug her but gets trapped in her chair because her bum is so big. This lightens the moment and makes Carron giggle.

'God, I wish I could cry like that. I'd get rid of all this water retention.'

Carron laughs out loud now, but she looks tired with tears and lack of sleep. She tells us how the children are doing and how she's making them feel as secure as possible. In the circumstances. And that Dennis has moved out and sees them every other weekend, but that he doesn't really know what to do with them when he has them. He would have preferred boys, she tells us. Dennis told her this when she gave birth.

'I've been to counselling with him but only to talk about the children. Mind you I don't trust him and don't want to be in the same room as him for more than a minute, as he uses every conversation, every opportunity to emotionally drag me down. They're only young, but the girls know what's happening. The counsellor said that I should say to the girls that Mummy and Daddy both love them and that it is nothing to do with them that we don't get on. That it's not their fault. It's Mummy and Daddy's fault that we messed up. She says that children tend to think that way, because they think they are the centre of the universe.'

'Of course I want to say that it's ninety-nine percent Daddy's fault because he's a selfish wanker and only one percent Mummy's fault as she tried to keep the marriage together, but you can't do that, can you.'

'And they'll know, Carron,' Doreen chips in. 'Children absorb situations by osmosis. You don't have to tell them things. They know. They will learn what their daddy is like as they grow up. Don't put him down in front of them, he will do the damage himself. Emily and Madeline are six and seven, aren't they?'

Carron nods yes. "It's a sensitive age, so I've got to be careful. They've both taken it badly and think it's their fault, hence reassuring them every day it isn't.' Bottom lip trembles again.

Everyone pauses for a sip of their drink. I switch the conversation to fluff. Literally.

'I gave myself a Brazilian a few weeks ago,' I say loudly, turning a few heads at neighbouring tables.

'What, a Brazilian man?' Valerie laughs.

'No, a Brazilian wax. You have a strip. A bit. I have an arrow pointing up.'

'Surely down would be better. You know, help men find their way and all that,' says Doreen playfully.

'I thought about having it pointing down but that means I've got to expose more and this way it's better the bottom's in the tail end of the arrow rather than at the point. If you know what I mean,' I say trying to explain without getting too explicit about it.

'Daniel gets more turned on if I don't shave,' Fran says matter-of-factly. 'He thinks it's more feminine to have something there so I have it trimmed.'

Carron says quietly, 'Well, I haven't looked down there for ages. I'm right off sex at the moment.'

'Me, too. Mind you, I can't even see mine,' Valerie says stroking her bump.

Looking down at her own crotch, then at me, Doreen asks, 'Do they still shave you there when you have a baby? I know they used to. I got a complete wax before I had my three simply because I didn't want some nurse shaving me when I felt and looked like shit.'

'They didn't do that to me, but it didn't seem to matter,' I reply.

'Did you have yours by caesarean or naturally?' asks Valerie.

'Naturally,' I say, trying not to sound smug.

'I never asked you, did you stretch a lot? Did you tear?' Doreen asks.

'You did ask me at the time, Doreen, I just didn't give you an answer as I was with David and some of his work colleagues at a banker's dinner party and they didn't seem to want to know about the bloody reality of childbirth over the beef Stroganoff. You also asked me if I ate my placenta.'

'Well, did you tear?' Doreen asks, turning other table heads again.

'No, didn't tear,' I say, trying to sound as though we're talking about opening envelopes rather than giving birth. 'Very lucky. No stitches. I wasn't induced. Made David have sex with me.'

''Full or oral?' Doreen asks, keeping the heads turned and mouths now open.

'Oral,' I say quietly, having given up on the envelope scam. 'And it worked.'

'Oh, I don't want Harry anywhere near me.' Valerie shudders. 'I'm scared he will damage the baby.'

I explain to Valerie that she should go on top. 'Men like that anyway because it's more weight bearing down on them and they feel more submissive and vulnerable. That's why men really like their women fat. It's like riding a moped, fun to ride but not sexy to be seen with.'

'Didn't he go off with a skinny ribs?' Doreen asks tactlessly, knowing the 'Charlotte' is skinny herself.

'Actually no, he went off with a girl who was quite plump and she lost lots of weight.'

'Perhaps she wanted to be more like you,' Doreen remarks.

'She had to fill her own shoes, Doreen. No one can fill mine. And no one will fill yours either, Carron. You are a very difficult act to follow and this girl, whatever her name is…' (I remember it but am not going to say it and even Doreen is not ruthless enough to remind me) '…has an impossible task. Dennis suffers from what most men suffer from. ME. You know. ME me me me me me me me me me me. Me, myself, I. She'll get to know that in time and she's got to make footprints of her own, because you are unique. And Dennis will realise that in two years, maybe five, maybe just before he cops it. By then, you'll be moved on. You don't think it now, but you will.'

'Everyone says that,' Carron murmurs.

'I know. Because it's true. I remember my counsellor saying that to me every time I saw her as though she wanted it to become my mantra. She said it would only work if I believed it. And eventually I did, and hey presto, here I am, with wonderful child, good health, lovely home and a job I love and find challenging and a fab set of friends in you all.'

Angus returns asking for our orders.

I play head girl.

Monkfish—a whole one—for Doreen, tuna for Carron and Fran, halibut for Valerie and I have the chicken. 'Do we want wine?' Yes, we all nod we do. Chardonnay, the one that Fran is having for her wedding. 'Water, a bottle of still and sparkling. Think that's about it.'

Over our food we talk about what we're planning to do for our respective birthdays. None of us have organised anything, though mine is the soonest—but I'm planning to be at home, with hopefully Sarah and me just celebrating. The girls think it would be good if we could go somewhere like EuroDisney where we can behave like kids. Valerie is scared she will get stuck in one of the rides, but Doreen assures her it's okay, and tells us she'll get Jane, her PA, to organise the event.

As we start to eat, Angus leans over to my ear and whispers, 'So what's this I hear about you dating a Brazilian guy ten years your junior?'

Chapter Ten
Joe Makes a Decision

'I've decided to tell her.'

'Tell her what?' Joe walks into my office without knocking on Monday morning at 8.30 a.m. carrying double espresso in one hand and *FT* in the other. My Monday mornings are always challenging, but recently they've become quite eventful.

'You've decided to tell her what?'

'That I want to separate and that we can't live together anymore. Do you mind me talking to you, Hazel?'

'Not at all, not at all. Please sit down.'

Joe sits down, drops *FT* on the floor and coffee on my desk. His hair looks slightly messy. And there's some stubble. Not usual solicitor look but I like it. Sort of a smarter version of Jamie Oliver. It quite suits him. He continues.

'I've been trying to deal with this with kindness and

thought I was being kind but don't think I was. You don't know much about me, Hazel, but I'm not a bad person and I didn't expect to meet you. I haven't been happy with Fiona for some time now but haven't done anything about it, because, well, because I love her, I'm just not in love with her any more. And we're good friends. And I was starting to feel, well, this is as good as it gets. And now, well, now, all her friends are getting married and having children and she's thirty-seven, and I know she wants to get married and have children and I was just plodding along and then I meet you. I meet you and, well, I don't know whether it would be kinder to stay or to go. And I don't know if I've been kind by staying all this time when I feel it wasn't right, or it would be kinder to leave now, or have left all those years ago.'

What can I say? What do I say to this man who looks very tired and stressed and like many of the clients I initially see on their first or second meeting with me about petitioning for divorce or having just received one.

'What are you going to do?'

'Well, I'll have to leave the house or she will. One of us has to leave. She'll be very distressed but she has family—a large family around her and this will help her. We also have mutual friends—a lot of them—and this also will help her, if not me.'

'Does she suspect you've met someone else?'

'I made the error of mentioning you a lot when I first joined the company. Believe it or not, in glowing terms, and I think that's why I got the impromptu meeting about lunch. She thinks you're lovely and, well, everything I said you were. She asked me direct if I was seeing you. I said no. She asked me if I had slept with you, I said no. She asked me if I had kissed you. She asked me a lot of questions. So although she may suspect I think she knows I wouldn't do that. But I feel guilty and I'm upset, but I can't stop thinking about you, Hazel. And I work with you. So it's not as if I can have a break from you. From seeing your face every morning. Hearing your voice. Being near you.'

I'm stunned, feeling sick again and with an incredible urge to get up, walk round the table and kiss him passionately on the lips and allow him to wrap his arms around my waist and pull me to him. But I don't, because I know it wouldn't be right, though it would feel right. I know that he has to sort his life out because I can't do it for him or become involved. I don't want him to offload his guilt or angst onto me because it's not fair. But because he's spoken the way he has, with the feeling he has for both Fiona's feelings and his own, I like him more. I, well, I more than like him.

'You've got to sort this out by yourself, Joe. I like you a lot. And yes, I think there is a chemistry between us. I thought initially it was just lust. Just chemistry—and that is difficult to work with, but then I've got to know you over the days and weeks and I like you. I enjoy being with you in and out of the courtroom. But I've met Fiona, and I know you think she doesn't know, but I think she does. I think she loves you very much and whatever you do now, it will break her heart. I know. I've been there. So be kind. Be honest and be kind. If it's a separation, don't say it's a trial separation and give her hope. Because she will hope. If you tell her now it's over, but there is no one else, you won't be lying. Not technically. And give yourself some space. Christ, after twelve years, you need space from a relationship to find your own identity again. What is true for a woman is also true of a man. You need that time. And so does she.'

'But I've wasted so much of her life. I haven't given her a child or married her. I haven't given her the security of either of those things. And as she mentioned to me a few times last night in tears, she'll be forty soon.'

'So what's wrong with being forty? I'm forty this year.'

'Yes, but you've been married. You've got a child and she hasn't. She's waited for me to make my mind up. And I have. And it's not to spend the rest of my life with her. And that's not kind.'

'Would staying with her, marrying her, having children, be kinder? Are you happy enough for that? You say you love her—is there enough love and friendship to make it last. If you have children, as you well know, it's different. You've got to think about things like this. You've got to think, Joe, about what would be kinder for her and for you. If you feel there is enough there to work on, you must work for it. If not, then you must go and tell her there is no turning back.'

'But I feel so guilty.'

'Then give her the house.'

'I don't feel that guilty.'

'Then don't give her the house. But make a decision.'

'I have. We're separating. I was thinking of asking you about how I should tell her it's over for good. But thought that inappropriate. You're not exactly the right person to bounce ideas off, are you?'

'Wrong person to bounce ideas off, Joe. All I will say is be self-deprecating when you do it. If you cry she'll either pity you or think you're pathetic and need mothering—neither outcome of which will help you or her. Don't say "I need space, feelings change, you could do better with someone else, you're too good for me, we don't talk any more, or I think of you as a sister". All of which may be true of course, but no girl, especially one you've been sleeping with for over twelve years, wants to hear it. Of course, you could start behaving like a twat, in which case she'll think "he's a twat, what did I ever see in him?", but it's been twelve years so she should know you inside out by now. Whatever you do don't tell her you like someone else. It's good she has a large family and good friends to go to, who are I hope are balanced, intelligent and will not goad her into either killing herself or killing you or cutting up your clothes. Don't try to be nice and don't get nasty. If you do it right she will hate you for about a year, may be a couple. If you get it wrong, she will hate you forever.'

'Oh, that's okay then. I feel much better. Must remember to ask you about all my personal problems.'

I smile. He looks stressed but he's brought this on himself. No one else has.

'You asked. I give advice on how to behave in matters of separation with as little blood as possible. There are no children involved, unless you can count your behaviour as childish, and I don't know about when she moved in and whose money is whose, but you know as well as I do all the ins and outs of situations like this as far as the technicalities are concerned.'

'I know.'

He turns to go. Then turns back.

'Can you do a drink after work today?'

'No, David is dropping off some boxes at the house. I said I would be in to collect them.'

Joe looks miffed that I'm, I suppose on the face of it, putting my ex before him, but I'm not, I've just made an arrangement and am sticking to it. And a drink with Joe at this time, when he's feeling this vulnerable is probably not a good thing. Vulnerability is very provocative in a man.

He turns and leaves again. I feel as though I've flattened him with my honesty, but I think it's for the best. I've tried to be as unconnected as possible, but it's difficult because I like and fancy Joe now, and that makes it difficult. I have an emotional attachment and the more I get to know him, the more I like him and the more I'm inclined to let my feelings get in the way of better judgement. Like wanting to give him space. Because at this moment I feel I'm on the edge of wanting to get to know him and don't want him to have space. Not from me anyway. And on top of that, all of that, I have compassion for Fiona. I know when he tells her, it may not come as a surprise, but it will be out in the open and when it's out there— the words are out there—'I want to separate, for good'— they hang there for days like a bad smell that won't go away. They take on a force of all their own so that any word of kindness or reason is always stained by the truth of wanting to go separate ways. She doesn't look hard or a bitch or arrogant or predatory. She looks nice. She looks gentle. She looks kind. Of course, if she knew what Joe and I almost did at the Pied Paella she would probably look very different—but this is understandable in the circumstances. Not that it would be easier if she looked nasty, but perhaps understandable why Joe doesn't feel he is in love with her any more. Perhaps it's just a transitory thing. Perhaps he's just nervous of committing and wants a last fling before he ties the knot and I'm the one. The chosen one. But I'm not that sort of girl. I'm not the last fling girl. And I'm starting to think Doreen is right. I do fucking pick 'em.

Chapter Eleven
Boxing Up the Past

Weak and controlling. I've decided the bulk of the male population are either one or both, but usually both. I don't base my analysis on cynicism or clinical research (although they are causes cited for most divorce petitions these days), but more gut feeling. My personal experience is based on hard fact. It is based on observing the words and actions of men and seeing how they differ, in most cases dramatically because (and they will offer a variety of reasons for this but the fundamental truth is) they are 'weak and/or controlling'. Okay, you say, gut feeling, what's the use of gut feeling? Listen to it and I think you can't go wrong. Women over forty that I've met have always told me they trust their gut feeling more rather than less as they age. Me, well, I ignored it over and over again at my cost. I don't think I'm alone. I know I'm not alone. I witness women ignoring their gut feelings every day. Most women realise this feeling or instinct has more to do with common sense. More to do with nurturing a sense of reality and wisdom. And it leaves most women sad and wary of the opposite sex, because the one thing I hate to hear, actually any woman hates to hear, is the excuse 'I was weak'. From anyone, but especially, especially, from their man.

That's the excuse David, ex of five years, partner for twenty-one years and official partner for eighteen years, gave me when he walked out. I would say, looking back, with a more objective eye, he was both weak and controlling. If that's possible. At the time, I didn't think it was. After all, if someone's weak, how can they be controlling? How can a woman, a strong woman like me, be controlled by a man who's weak? Agh, you see, there's the rub. I loved him. I was weak. Now I'm using it. I'm using that excuse. I was weak. Two weak people together. Disaster. My cousin Helen didn't think he was weak. She just thought he was a wanker. She would tell me, 'Hazel, Hazel, you are a wanker magnet. Any wanker from a mile off will smell you out and want to make you his own. They see your energy and they think aha (I always imagined some Terry Thomas-cum-Brad Pitt-like creation swooping down on me in black cloak and whisking me off to his castle tower when she said this. Not always altogether totally unpleasant thought depending if I was feeling horny or not at the time). They think aha, I will take you as my own, sap all your strength, totally confuse you and wham bam, make you think all my guilt is your guilt, all my stuff is now your stuff, and what's more, it's your fault that I'm so weak and controlling. You bring it out in me. You bring the weakness out in me.' And he said I brought out the worst in him. Yes, I would say, hand on heart, I definitely brought the very worst out in David.

David was my Terry Thomas/Brad Pitt creature, although he had none of the humour of Terry nor sexual charisma of Brad Pitt. I liked him because I thought he was cute. Now I think about it, if I find a man cute, I am highly suspicious of my own motives, and focus on the wisdom of knowing I just want to sleep with them. Ideally without getting emotionally involved, which of course is impossible, because I'm a woman. I'm weak. See, there it is again. That ruddy word. I'm weak. Sorry, I hit her, I'm weak. Sorry, I married her, and didn't love her, because I didn't want to hurt her, I'm weak. Sorry, I slept with him, the passion, the sexual energy was overpowering, I'm weak. I don't think I have met a strong person in all my working or personal life. Certainly not a man. My friends, Doreen, Valerie, Fran, even downtrodden Carron, I think they're strong. But David, David who I stayed with, had a child with and divorced very acrimoniously but financially well, is probably the weakest, most controlling man I ever and have ever met. I would let him decide how long I would speak to people at parties (half an hour to any man was far too long) and he has this pet phrase, 'call me old-fashioned', which translates as I'm a control freak. I know it does, that's not gut instinct, that's based on personal as well as professional experience. All control freaks say it.

I am meeting 'call me old-fashioned' David today, because he has found some of my old stuff (actual rather than emotional, I hope) and needs to deliver it to me. It's too big and heavy to send through the post. I've suggested he bins it, but he thinks there may be things I would like to keep. Old photos. Of us. I think perhaps Sarah would like to keep them. I tore the wedding album up on the morning after he stayed out all night with his girlfriend and failed to turn up to counselling. I told Fran it felt good at the time. She said it probably did but that it was a shame for Sarah. I said the whole ceremony had been made a sham and its hypocrisy reeked through every frame. God, I was angry then. Bloody difficult to tear those books. They bind them well. I'm only sorry for the pages with photos of my dad, and mum, who I like to remember. Neither of them lived long enough to witness the breakup, which is for the best. I felt at the time, they were looking down on me, in my loneliness, sobbing silently inside, they wanted to take all the pain from me. My father would always tell me he wished he could take my pain, so I wouldn't have to bear it. He couldn't of course, but I know, every time he said it, he meant it. He would always say the right words. My mother on the other hand had a habit of biting her lip (literally, she would make it bleed sometimes, I think it was some sort of nervous disorder), but failed to bite her lip and speak when she shouldn't. She wouldn't engage brain before opening mouth. Ever. She would take on the sympathy rather than the pain. Think they call it transference, but whatever it was called, it pissed me off when she told me everyone felt sorry for her. Why should they feel sorry for her? So perhaps it was a good thing she wasn't here to give advice during my time with David, because I would have probably topped myself on the basis of listening to her advice. Of course, I loved them both. Just I missed my dad so much more. So much more.

David arrives at ten in his blue convertible 3 series BMW with electric roof. He is wearing a black jumper and black chinos and attitude. Both of us look so much more attractive since we split up, we both look at each other these days, and rather than think what did I ever see in them, think why didn't they look that good when I went out with them. Of course, we answer ourselves. We didn't look this good because we were both dreadfully unhappy. And it showed. And I can always tell when I walk down a street now and look at couples, their body language, those who are genuinely happy and those who just pretend to be. I would say, a good ninety-five percent on any street on London are as miserable as sin according to my analysis. But I may be wrong. Perhaps it's just that gut feeling again.

'Right, there's two boxes. I think stuff that Sarah would like.'

'Fine, I'll put them in the loft. See if she can find time to look through them, she's so busy these days.'

'Yes, well, college and all that (slight pause), how are you?'

So simple that, isn't it, being asked 'how are you?' I would love to say I'm really well, I'm happy, have a potential new man in my life, am dancing about with joy inside (not that he'd really care or want to know that bit) and am altogether the happiest I've been in a long time and am looking forward to turning forty. I don't. I don't say any of these things because I know, I've come to know, that David still harbours anger and resentment and bitterness and it comes out when he learns or hears anything about me that remotely resembles contentment. For a start, I pissed him off something rotten when I did better at work after we split up. Our last remaining mutual friends told me so. It also annoyed him when I started dating men who were not only taller (not hard—he scrapes five foot eleven though he lies about his height), more handsome (he chose someone who was physically less attractive than me), and stronger, as he couldn't intimidate them when we met. In fact, the reverse used to happen. But I didn't want to make David cross, because when he was cross (I prefer the word cross to angry, it's somehow less dark), he got nasty. Not in a childish, stamp feet, bang head against table sort of way. He got nasty in a very calculated way. He possessed a book of all my faux pas over the years—from the most insignificant 'didn't cook pasta right' to the more seminal 'had an affair with a photographer'. I know he does, because when Sarah was fifteen, he showed it to her. She cried a lot, returned from that particular weekend and it was horrible for about a month, but when I spoke to her about the hows and whys, without damning her father (God I worked hard on my mantra 'may he be happy may he be well' that month), she said she understood that it must have been intolerable for both of us, and I said, yes it was, and that I still loved her father, and I never alas kept such a book about him. It would have been a library—but I didn't tell her that bit.

He also used to gently suggest to Sarah every time he saw her that she would be happier living with him and his girlfriend than with me. He knew that the courts wouldn't allow it, and so thought if he could work on her, that she would make the decision, but I always allowed Sarah to meet her dad when she wanted to, speak to him when she wanted to, and tried to be the best mother I could be, not only because I love Sarah, and wanted her to grow up happy and healthy and balanced, but because I knew David and his parents (bless their little Irish Catholic hypocritical socks) would fight for custody and use anything to prove I was an unfit mother. He once told me, very quietly after dropping Sarah off, and asking for a quick chat, he whispered, 'You know, Hazel, I don't wish you dead. I know you think I do, but I don't. I wish you a long life, so I can see how miserable I can make you for the rest of your life. I take great pleasure from that knowledge'. He whispered this, and smiled at me, handed me a CD of *Madame Butterfly* with a Post-it attached saying *think about it,* and turned and went and I felt quite sick. I think I threw up. I couldn't even cry that time. I didn't tell anyone about it for a long time. I just put it in the back of my mind, binned the CD and tried to forget it. It came out when I spoke to Angie one time and she said over time the 'wrong' voices would disappear. Both my mother's and David's.

But the thing that most annoyed David was that he couldn't control me any more. Well, he could in some ways. With money he would delay payments so I had to contact everyone to let them know the payment would be delayed on that month's instalment and he would always pay just before court proceedings were issued which meant unnecessary expense and worry which he again, always whispered to me, that he enjoyed. Then of course, he tried to get to me emotionally via Sarah, but I wasn't one of his possessions any more and he regarded everything he, as he put it, 'paid for', as his possession. Of course, all his friends, who were our friends when we were together (but were all bankers so were ultimately neither of our friends) thought he was lovely. He has, I admit, many lovely ways, but they don't make up for the dark side. He's not so much Terry Thomas and Brad Pitt, more Darth Vader meets Uriah Heep. But to any layman on first meeting he comes across as so charming, so balanced, so sane, and he's not. He's a nutter and while I was married to him, I think he started to make me doubt my own sanity. So when this English Psycho asks me how I am, I say, 'Fine.'

And leave it at that. Not because I'm not friendly, or bitter, or afraid, or angry. Just because it's the only safe thing to say to someone who's this messed up and calculatedly malicious.

Unfortunately, David wants to talk. I know this because he lingers when I want to close the door.

'You're turning forty this year, aren't you?'

What do I say to this? If I say yes, it's too open. It allows him to say something else, but how can I close it. If I say no, it's next year, he may have asked Sarah, and will put my memory loss down to insanity and note this in his book, using it as evidence that I'm an unfit mother (I'm not paranoid honestly, I know David would do this because he said he would three years ago if I ever forgot how old I was. Yes, really). If I say maybe, then it suggests it is something I would prefer to forget (I don't) and so any comment would fall on deaf ears. So I say, 'Maybe.'

He looks amused.

'Any man on the scene then?'

I don't have to think on this one. I know how he'll react to any possibility of yes or maybe (more comments to Sarah, bringing up memories of separation bullying), so I'm hardly likely to talk about Joe, younger, taller, brighter, more handsome, (I hope) kinder.

'No.'

He smiles again. 'Oh well, shit happens.'

I say nothing. I don't wish him well or say goodbye or anything that might be misinterpreted as conversation. I close the door quietly as he turns and think if Joe ever, but ever says to me 'call me old-fashioned' or 'I'm weak' I will run a mile.

I leave the boxes in the hallway for a few hours before I decide to look through and see what the important stuff is that David thinks I should keep for Sarah. I make some tea, then coffee, play The Cure and Jim Morrison, and then pick up the first box and nest in front of the mock Adams-style fireplace and sift. When David and I split, I destroyed all of the photos of him and me together I could find. Those with him and Sarah I gave to him, and I have the ones of Sarah and me together. I do not have one single memento or photo or memory of David in the house. Apart from Sarah that is, which is the best thing we ever did for each other. I lie, I have a necklace with a single pearl, rubies and diamonds that David presented to me when I gave birth to Sarah. It's exquisite and I keep it because I want to pass it on to Sarah one day. Not necessarily if and when she gets married, just one day. When I feel it's appropriate.

I don't recognise myself in the photos I see before me. He must have taken some of me when he took those of Sarah and himself. I expect he threw darts at them but, inspecting them closely, I can't see any pin marks. Perhaps he did the voodoo thing with the doll and strands of hair, but I'm still in one piece at the moment. So perhaps not. My hairstyle looks so weird. Tight and bobbed and heavily highlighted. More like a bad block colour of dandelion blond, but I have the same round face and smile. Although the smile looks forced. I don't smile like that these days. The eyes in the photos are sad. The mouth smiles. The eyes are sad, or perhaps I just see something in them that isn't there. Perhaps. And at least I don't wear light blue eye makeup that many of my friends wore in those days. I'm wearing suits and ill-fitting blouses and no bra (because I didn't think I needed one, but I did), and I look very uncomfortable. In all the photos it's as though I'm not staring at myself from another time, it's another person. I'm not this person any more. This is someone pretending to be me. A much weaker, insecure, vulnerable and unsure girl, who's yet to form as a person. Not someone my friends or Joe would recognise. Not me. Not me at all.

There are photos of drinks parties, and the time David dressed up with friends in black tie and dark glasses, a group of bankers called the Guinness Eight—although nine invariably turned up for the piss-up—and the girls all wore little black dresses and mine was particularly little because I was at the anorexic stage of our relationship when I didn't want to feel anything—anger, passion, lack of it, resentment, sadness—and not eating helped. And I can barely recognise Hazel Chamberlayne in any of these photos either. It's a bit like a scene from the *Twilight Zone*. Someone's showing me photos of myself and I don't recognise them. It's a bit creepy. There are photos of our honeymoon. Must bin those. And the time we went to Disney World in the States. That was good. That was before we got married. I remember being very happy then. It wasn't all bad—our relationship. Perhaps I should suggest Benson do a similar thing, although I think he's ceremonially burnt all the images of Mrs Benson but perhaps in time, in ten years or twenty years' time, he may think differently. Perhaps.

Perhaps Sarah should keep these after all. I have some for Sarah already, but it's unfair of me not to let her see them. So I don't bin anything. I think if her dad wants her to have these, then I should let her sift through herself. But deep down, I hope she looks through and bins the lot—especially the ones of David grinning inanely at me, as if to say, you can't escape, you can't escape. I did darling, I did, thank goodness.

When Sarah comes in I tell her about the boxes.

'Oh, I'll look when I've got time, Mum. I'd prefer to look together if that's okay with you. Then we can decide what we want to keep and what we want to chuck.'

'They're for you, Sarah.'

'I know, but, well, the memories weren't good ones. They're the past, and they should stay there.'

'They weren't all bad.'

'I know they weren't all bad, but I don't need reminding of them. And neither do you. They'll always be with you and Dad and one day, when I'm older I'll look, but not yet. Keep them in the loft and I'll look at them one day. But not now. Are you planning anything for your birthday, Mum?'

'Maybe going to EuroDisney with the girls, but apart from that, no.'

'Right, okay, then, I'll cook dinner for you on your birthday—just the two of us—okay?' She beams with a twinkle in her eye.

'That would be lovely.'

As I put the boxes in the loft that evening, I think how

I've dealt with my fears and pain and anger, and if I've just bottled it all up and put it in boxes which may explode at any time, like Benson. I don't think so. I think I've dealt with my stuff okay. Perhaps I'll explode on the day I turn forty as I'm told some women do. When all their past achievements and failures flash before their eyes and they think 'what have I done?'. But climbing down from the loft, I'm pretty cool about everything. I'm not in denial about getting older, getting more wrinkles (which I see as character—why anyone wants Botox I don't know. Who wants to go round looking like a startled rabbit all the time?) or getting any of those other physical ailments women over forty suffer from. I'll take it in my stride, with grace and humour I hope, much as I do everything these days. I want to prepare an action list of things I want to do before my forty-first birthday though. Ten things that will stretch and challenge me. It's strange, as I put all the memories, some good, some bad in the loft to be taken down who knows when, I feel less boxed in than ever. The little girl in the photos looked afraid of life and herself and her sexuality and her boyfriend, who later became her husband. Perhaps the old Hazel should stay in the box. This Hazel thinks out of it these days.

Chapter Twelve
Getting to Know Joe

'I don't need counselling!' Benson screams at Joe.

Mr Benson is screaming at Joe, who is managing to hold back the laughter or anger—can't work out which emotion.

Joe has just suggested Mr Benson might be helped if he went to see a counsellor for anger management.

'Outbursts in court about the judge are not a good idea,' Joe says calmly.

''The bloke was a fucking wanker,' Benson replies, snorting like some enraged horse.

'Telling him this is not a good idea,' says Joe. 'I am sure even you realise this, Mr Benson.'

'I realise this, but honestly, the decision to investigate further into my affairs—is that really necessary? Can't you stop them from doing this?'

'No,' replies Joe.

'I've managed to hide—'

I interrupt Benson. I don't want him to tell us something that prejudices his case. 'May I remind you, Mr Benson, anything you tell us we are obliged to reveal to the court and Mrs Benson's solicitors. So please keep this in mind when you are telling us anything.'

'Oh right. Right.'

He stops shouting and thinks for a bit. Smiles and sits down.

Benson ponders. 'So you think counselling would help me?'

'I think so,' says Joe. 'It's helped many of our clients.'

'And she can't say I'm nuts because I'm going to a counsellor?' Benson asks more calmly.

'On the contrary, Mr Benson, it shows you are a responsible human being and furthermore, responsible father.'

'Right.'

He thinks again. Head in hands. 'Right, so do you recommend anyone?'

'We have a list of qualified counsellors we can recommend,' I say. 'I think you will find they will be very helpful. Not only with your anger, but also other anxieties you may have. Anger may only be the symptom of issues, not the cause.'

'That fucking bitch was the cause of my anxieties. *Is* the cause of my anxieties. I can tell you that. I don't need a fucking counsellor to tell me that.'

'Here is a list. I have starred those ones I think most appropriate. We don't have another court appearance for at least another six weeks, so I suggest you organise an initial meeting and see if you can see them on a regular basis. About two times a week possibly.'

'Will it cost a fortune?'

'It may end up saving you a lot of money if you are able to control yourself in court, Mr Benson,' I say, offering him a cup of water as he's demolished the previous one.

Mr Benson calms down. He stands and shakes hands with both of us, then leaves the meeting room muttering, 'Kill Gill, Kill Gill, Kill Gill.' Obviously, his wife's first name.

I return to my office and close the door. And smile at Joe, who is smiling back at me. We haven't been able to talk about anything personal since we spoke in this office last week. I don't know if he's moved out of the house, or she's moved out of the house, or they're back together again or what. So I ask, 'How are you?'

'Okayish,' he says, slumping down into my chair. 'We've had lots of talks. She's stronger than I thought she was. She's agreed to move out rather than me, which I feel bad about. She says she loves me and wants me back the way I was when we first met.'

I smile. I remember saying those words to David all those years ago.

'I think she feels let down. She knows it hasn't been right for some time. I tried to break it up last year, but there were so many tears I thought I would try to make it work, but it hasn't been right. And then I met you.'

'So I'm a catalyst. But you're not leaving her for me, are you? This puts an emotional burden on me that I don't need or want.'

'No, I was unhappy in my relationship, but you do have something to do with my actions. Why I'm doing it now.'

'Does she suspect you like me?'

'She hasn't asked any more about you. She said when she met you that you'd be the sort of woman I'd go for.'

I smile. 'What sort of woman is that?'

'You fishing for compliments, Ms Chamberlayne? She was very sweet about you, Hazel, which only made it worse. We have history—twelve years of it and a lot of it has been good.'

'Then why don't you try to make a go of it, Joe? Do you still love her?'

'Yes, I do, but I'm not in love with her and I can't change the way I feel. And it's not just because of you, it's been there a long time. I have tried to fall in love with her again, but it didn't work. And I thought I was being kind by staying, but I'm not. I went to a wedding last month. Her best friend was getting married in Devon. And it just polarised the whole issue. The fact I was so unhappy. Am so unhappy. I wanted to text you or call you from the reception and I'd just met you. Think I'd been here a week and I thought, hey, if I ring you, you'll think I'm nuts. And now, I'm excited about you. About, well, the possibility of us.'

'I understand. And I understand about the history. At least you can make a new history for yourself, and so can she. You don't have children, so you can give each other space and there isn't a constant reminder of the good and bad times beaming away at you each day, like I had with Sarah. You see, I understand how Fiona feels. I was her once. I understand her feelings of betrayal and loss and bereavement. If she genuinely felt you'd left her for another woman, she'd feel angry and you might see a different side to her. So to save her pride and your reputation—I'm sure you don't want to be perceived by mutual friends as having gone from one relationship straight to another—I suggest you spend time by yourself for a few months.'

'Or keep our relationship a secret.'

'It doesn't work that way, Joe. And with all due respect, I don't want to be a secret. She will find out, and you need time by yourself. It will give you time to deal with your baggage, rather than, well, offloading onto me or whoever happens to come along.'

'It's going to be difficult.'

'I know. We work together. We see each other every day. We're going to New York together soon. We should both try to be professional. No kissing, no sex, no guilt.'

'I feel guilty and I haven't done anything. I haven't even kissed you.'

'But you've thought about it and that's why you're feeling guilty. Not Catholic, are you?'

'No, just human.'

He smiles and leaves me wondering how professional and restrained I can be with him in the office, and allow him the space he needs now. Perhaps for New York I should leave the La Perla at home, after all.

Chapter Thirteen
Of Mice and Men

Sheryl Crowe's all-time greatest single girl's anthem blares from my personal CD player. Music conjures up moments in my life like nothing else. 'Oh Come All Ye Faithful' was playing outside my hospital room as I gave birth to Sarah. 'Nobody Does it Better' by Carly Simon, theme tune to *The Spy Who Loved Me,* when David proposed and 'I Hate You So Much Right Now' by I can't remember who, though she did sound very annoyed, was my theme tune for a few years after we got divorced. Sheryl's tune reminds me of a lover from my past. A particularly wonderful one. Of furtive fumblings in the passenger seat of his car as he drove me home, trying to concentrate on an endless road, but occasionally catching sight of my teasing lit by the moonlight and occasional street lamps. Of that sick lustful yearn-ing. That feeling I now have for Joe. Joe, bless him, has Billy Joel's 'New York State of Mind.' No matter. I'm sure it will pass.

The five of us are on a train going to EuroDisney for the day. No men. Just the girls with over twenty-four hours of chat inside them. We are hoping Valerie doesn't give birth but if it's going to be born, there are worse places than EuroDisney. Perhaps she'll call it Daisy or Minnie. Valerie scowls at the thought and tells us politely to fuck off. We've decided to stay the night in the Disneyland Hotel, onsite, so we get to go in an hour before the park opens to the plebs. The girls all want a fluffy Mickey Mouse, except me, who's always felt Donald got a really bad press and needed love. So I'm buying one of him and a Daisy for Joe. Now isn't that naff.

'Don't be so anti-social and get those earplugs out and talk to us', shouts Doreen over Sheryl. I do as I'm told.

'Now who's bought the champagne? Has anybody bought the champagne?' Doreen shouts down the carriage as the girls climb on board with bottles of the pink stuff and Marks & Spencer best of range.

'I have!' yells Carron. 'I've got the champagne. Think Fran's got the food. What have you got, Valerie?'

'If I don't sit down soon, probably contractions,' replies Valerie. 'Have you booked two seats for me, Doreen?'

'No, but it's pretty empty in this carriage. We're travelling business so they're wider anyway, but you can have one all to yourself.'

'I will need one all to myself.'

'Fine,' shouts Doreen. 'You sit there. Fran, bring the food here. Hazel, Carron, you okay?'

'Yeah, we're okay,' I say.

Carron tells us she's met someone. He's a friend of Dennis. Or was a friend of Dennis. He's not now as he's sleeping with Carron. He's not married, but she's fancied him for a long time. He's divorced with four children, grown up, own business and has been very sweet according to Carron. 'He said he got to know the real me ironically when Dennis was talking about me, and he saw what a wanker, as he called him, Dennis had been, and decided to call me and ask if he could be of help.'

Doreen smiles. 'And he obviously was.'

Carron smiles. 'Obviously.'

We're all pleased Dennis's ex-friend has put a smile back on Carron's face. I know in two years Carron will be in a much better place emotionally than she is now. Fran says she won't mention the wedding preparations for the duration of the trip as it's starting to bore even her, so that's all fine.

Methinks I dislike *maid of honour* though. Sounds like a poshed-up version of old maid. I'd rather be called a train adjuster, or a flower holder, or something. Maid of honour sounds old. There are some things which make you sound older even when you're not. And maid of honour is one of them. Like Spinster. I ask the girls if they've done a list of all those things they want to do before they're fifty. Because I have.

Doreen says she hasn't but that it's a good idea. She gets

a notebook out and writes FIFTY MUST-DOS. BE-
FORE.

I get my list of must-dos and read aloud.

1. Must write a book of erotic fiction and get it published.
2. Must get house in Tuscany.
3. Must get through 40s without plastic surgery or
Botox and look as though haven't.
4. Must read all Booker Prize winners for the past
20 years (have promised myself this since I was 20).
5. Must learn Italian and French fluently.
6. Must learn to ride well.
7. Must learn to ski well.
8. Must learn to surf well.
9. Must learn to dive well.
10. Must learn to love well.

I look up and see their faces.

'Well, that's a nice mix of the material, spiritual, aspi-
rational, emotional and downright ridiculous. You want
to achieve them in that order?' Fran asks. 'Is that their order
of importance or order in which you thought of them?'

'Thought of the material, the experiences, the fanta-
sies and then the spiritual.'

'Don't you want to have another child?'

'No,' I say.

'All the things seem very selfish. There's nothing with
Joe in there. Or men in there.'

'Learning to love well. That's him really.'

'That could be anyone. How about getting married or being less self-centred.'

'Fran, what's come over you?'

'Oh, I don't know. Maybe I'm jealous. I see you all and you're enjoying life and you don't have a man. Well, you do have a man, but you're not tied down. You don't have any ties and I'm getting married and all I think about it is that I'm getting responsibilities and not only that, I will have to compromise. I don't feel my life is beginning, I feel it's narrowing and this is what I've wanted, put on my action list since I was ten and now, well, I don't think I want it. I love Daniel, don't get me wrong, I do. But I thought about what Doreen said over lunch at Le Pont, about marriage being no more than a contract.'

'Oh, ignore me, darling. I come out with such crap sometimes.'

'No, you don't, Doreen, you do sometimes, but not then. Marriage is no more than a legal contract, you yourself know that, Hazel. You deal with this particular contract every day and get both parties to read the small print they failed to do when they signed it. As for the spiritual side, no one believes in God any more. More people believe in the Church than God, which is ever so slightly hypocritical so why I'm getting married in a church is beyond me, because, well, I believe in God, but I don't have any time for the church or religion. And neither does Daniel. That's one of the reasons I love him. He has no hypocrisy in him whatsoever. But by doing this, by marrying this way, well, it is hypocritical.'

I look at Fran. She is going through what I know every woman goes through usually a month, sometimes the year before she gets married. Her last year of being single. The year of doubt and temptation and have I done the right thing and do I want to be with this man, faithful to this man for ever. And will he be good for me as well as to me. Fran is so levelheaded, so grounded, I thought she would have dealt with this and moved on, but she seems to be stuck. Perhaps it's because she's got close friends who're going through divorce, a best friend who's a divorce lawyer, and is turning forty, a seminal age by anyone's standards. So I say, 'These are last-minute nerves. Everyone has them. You're getting married in a month's time and I know at the moment you probably feel as though you've been duped for most of your life by society into thinking this, this walking down the aisle thing, is what it's all about. Well, it's not, but in my view, marriage is, or has become another box into which you neatly put companionship and friendship and sex. Ultimately, it's what you want it to be—not what someone else says it might be. As long as you agree on what it means to both of you, that's fine. Screw everyone else's opinion. It's your and Daniel's that matters.'

'I'm older and wiser. I should know better.'

'Do you think with age comes wisdom?' I ask, thinking of Sarah and Joe. 'I used to think that. But age brings a rigidity to thought sometimes—a narrow-mindedness when it should broaden over time. We think we know best, when in fact, we don't. We get set in our ways thinking they're the best ways—the tried and tested ways—but they're not. They're just easier and tired and relate to a different time that's no longer relevant. With age comes experience, but we only gain from it ultimately if we learn from it. You love Daniel. I know you do. These are just last-minute nerves.'

'I've got another four weeks. I can always say no on the day, or not turn up.'

'Whatever you do, don't tell us. Coz he will grill us afterwards about knowing or not knowing and why didn't we tell and stuff.'

'I'll leave you all in suspense as to if I'll turn up on the day. Okay?'

'Okay.'

For some reason, I'm quite excited about the prospect of Fran making the wedding day a possible, not a definite. It will happen of course. But could it go on without the bride? I've been to some weddings where the bride seemed almost superfluous. She was there in body, but not in spirit, said nothing, just shook hands and laughed at the groom's, best man's and her father-in-law's jokes. Oh, get real, Hazel, I'm talking about my experience of wedding day. Fran's will be different. She will be the focal point. She will be the reason we are all there. For her sake.

'So what does everyone think of my action list and has anyone done one of their own?'

Everyone shakes their heads.

'I've done all I want to do,' explains Doreen. 'I don't want to travel anywhere I haven't been to. Or get higher in my career.'

The tannoy on the train announces we're going through the tunnel. I get the champagne out and pour for each of us.

Valerie sighs. 'I just want to let my fortieth come and go without me making a song and dance about it. I don't want anything special.'

'The date and day are like any other,' I say. 'But I think its best to think about it before it happens rather than deal with the aftermath, which is what I think a lot of people—not just women—men, too—do as well. All those men who have played the field, may have reached the peak of the corporate ladder and think, hey, I don't have a wife. Lots of other trophies and no wife and no heir and spare and I gotta get them quick. I see that a lot these days. They collect families like they collect everything else. Did you know, the latest trend amongst the city slickers is having three families in one lifetime?'

'Bit greedy, isn't it?' Fran comments.

'I suppose you could argue it's as nature intended. Males roam from family to family. That's what they do in the wild. They spread their seed.'

Fran interrupts. 'Perhaps Henry VIII got it right. Ask yourself, who out of all his missus got the best deal? Was it Number One or Number Six? The one who got the young man, emotionally immature, full of hope and energy, enthusiasm and pride or the one who got the old, tired, having learnt nothing from any of the experience of course, holding onto the anger and resentment and power to behead?'

Doreen smiles. 'Surely the wives who didn't get beheaded, who survived the experience, got the best deal.'

'Well, yes, if you think of marriage as an experience to survive as opposed to one to thrive on. But my point is I think each wife essentially has the same man. Different body, slightly more wrinkled package, but same man who followed the same pattern. The older man is harder work, with more baggage, yet still with the mind of a selfish boy. That's why I think it's best to get the man young, because you get the man at twenty and they'll be that way at forty and at sixty, only they won't move as fast.'

'I suppose men could say that about women,' adds Valerie.

'They often do. Difference is, women learn from their experiences and they enjoy maturing emotionally. That's why there aren't as many female Peter Pans, as there are male. In my experience, most men don't learn about life while they're living it, whereas most women do.'

We all then discuss the things we've done in our lives of which we're most proud. With the exception of Valerie, who's expecting her first, and Fran, who's yet to marry, we all say having children. Even Doreen, who I thought would say career, says having her brood comes way ahead of getting CEO.

'I know you all thought I would say career, but it

doesn't compare with having kids. I like being a mum. I enjoyed being a mum a lot more than I do being a wife and I think hand on heart you ask most women and they'll say the same thing. I think those who don't have children in the end treat their husbands like kids or get cats or dogs and treat them like kids, but they must have this maternal relationship with something or someone even if it ends up being the house plant or the postman.'

The girls sit and stare at Doreen as though she's said something deeply profound. I think she's simply voiced what all of us think. Doreen's career gives her drive and energy, her husband support, but it's her kids that inspire her. Not her husband. Not her marriage.

Thanks to my bullying everyone has taken hand luggage only. Here for two days, one night in the Disneyland Hotel, we all feel slightly heady but happy. A very premenstrual Daisy Duck greets us at reception and asks us in strangled English if we have our passports. Doreen takes the lead.

'Girls. All passports please.'

We hand all passports to head girl.

We're sharing rooms. And I'm the odd one out for some reason. Doreen says it's because I smell. We've done lunch on the train, so we head for Fantasyland.

Doreen snarls, 'I don't want to do that fucking Small World ride. Elephants fine. Either I queue for them with Valerie or go on the Indiana Jones thing, but I'm not doing that ride.'

Valerie wants to do the haunted house. I tell her she

can do what she likes. I want to do the Peter Pan ride and Space Mountain, while Carron wants to see if they have a Johnny Depp puppet at the *Pirates of the Caribbean*. I say I doubt it.

Two hours and four rides later, we've done Fantasyland and Discoveryland. And some of Wild West Land. Well, we think it's Wild West land but they call it something else in the brochure. Valerie gets stuck in the elephant and is helped out by three burly French Chipmunks that she liked. Fran falls in the water at the *Pirates of the Caribbean* trying to collect a souvenir from one of the pirates, who looks a teensy bit like J Depp. And fails. Doreen threw something at one of the dolls in Small World ride and is banned from going on the boats again. A feat of which she is extremely proud. She quotes something from a Monty Python film about the French official's mother drinking elderflower wine. Or something. Anyway, she says it in French so it sounds even funnier. Think we're all still pissed.

8:00 p.m. and fireworks. I get my purse pinched. Bloody French. Doreen tells me they could have been English. I think this is a possibility as ninety-nine percent of people who come to EuroDisney are English, despite the fact that everything is written in French and said in French, at least initially.

9:00 p.m. and Wild West Show where we watch the Bison being chased by the Indians being chased by the cowboys and we discuss how badly the First Nations are being treated by the American government and how the land should still belong to the Indians and how a lot of modern medicine emanates from their ideals. And the little boy behind us, who can't hear what is going on and can't be more than twelve, tells us to shut the fuck up. I think he has a point.

10:00 p.m. and we're knackered. Valerie wants to go to bed because she's sleeping for two. Fran wants to go to bed because she still feels queasy. Doreen and Carron are still debating if giving head is sex or not. I say of course it fucking is.

I put my head down on the Minnie Mouse pillow case and have nightmare of dolls at the Small World ride chasing me with litigation papers.

Chapter Fourteen
Valerie Has the Baby

Knock on door in middle of night. Half awake. It's Fran.

'What's the matter?'

'It's Valerie, she's bleeding. I've called the receptionist but there's no one there that can speak good English. Hazel, your French is up to scratch, we've got to do something, she's in agony.'

I don't talk. I put a dress on as I'm walking down the corridor with Fran.

'Have you woken the others?'

'No, not yet.'

'Get them up. And get Carron and Doreen to stay with her. I will go to reception.'

I rush to the reception desk. The morose Daisy has been replaced by a sleepy Donald. I say in my best French,

'One of your guests is having a baby in Room 209. I need an ambulance NOW.'

The duck understands. And calls for an ambulance.

I tell the duck if the girl dies I am a solicitor and will sue it for manslaughter. And that Lady Diana would have lived if she'd had that car crash in England instead of France.

Ambulance arrives in twenty minutes. Valerie able to walk, still bleeding. Girls all suddenly look much older than forty. And feel it, I can tell. I go in ambulance. The others take a taxi. The French streets are buzzing. Buzzing is now in my head. Valerie is just whimpering.

'The baby will be all right, won't it?'

'Yes, Valerie, it will be all right. It will be all right. I will call Harry. It will be all right. You're over eight months. That's good. And look at the size of you. He or she must be huge. Just wants to have a French passport and can you blame him?'

'Yes, that must be it. That must be it.'

At hospital, they take her in on a trolley and I follow. One person, who looks like a doctor, asks if I'm a relative.

'Yes, I'm her sister. My other sisters are in the taxi.'

The doctor allows us to go in the room with her. I ask the doctor if I can help. He asks me how far gone she is. I reply eight months and say that I don't think she's had any problems and that she's nearly forty and isn't allergic to penicillin or anything in particular to my knowledge. And that she doesn't like hospitals, but he doesn't seem to get the joke.

Others arrive. Looking frazzled. Doreen tells me no one brought their fucking purses, did they? So she had to find a cash point in the middle of the night. And asks how Valerie is and has she had the baby yet.

I say no.

So we sit. And think about life and friendship and ourselves and each other and how helpless we are. How helpless. Useless. Incompetent. Sipping tar-thick espresso from the machine. Good to know coffee in hospitals even in France is disgusting. National Health can't be blamed for everything.

Doctor comes out.

Smiling. It's a girl. 'Mother and baby doing fine. Would you like to see her?'

Collective 'yes please.' Collective grinning at baby and mummy, who's all tearful and looks even more knackered than her sisters. Baby looks red and puffy and squashed but we all insist she's perfect and has a perfect-shaped head and is beautiful because she is. She's Valerie's baby and she's beautiful.

Valerie asks me if anyone has called Harry and I say 'shit, no, but will do that straight away.' She gives me his number. I rush outside, switch on mobile and dial, not forgetting code.

A very tired voice answers, 'Hello, who's that?'

'Hazel, it's Hazel. Valerie's had the baby. It's a girl. We're in the hospital in Paris.'

'Oh my God! Oh my God! Oh, I wasn't there with her. Can I speak to her?'

Man crying down the phone.

'I can't use the phone in the hospital. She's okay. She's okay and the baby is okay and looks nothing like you, Harry.'

'I hope not. Hope she's got her mother's looks. Oh my God. I've got to get over there. Get a flight.'

'Yes, she'll be here a few days I would think. Go on the Net, you'll get one quick. Or come by train.'

'Right. I'll do that. Train now. Right now. Oh my God.'

'And, Harry.'

'Yes?'

'Well done, Daddy.'

Man crying down phone again.

'Oh right. Yes. Oh God. Trust Valerie to have it in France. She'll want to call her Paris I should think.'

'Better than Brooklyn.'

'Definitely. Definitely.'

Return to mother and baby and three doting friends, all of whom are completely hyper with caffeine and admiration. I tell Valerie I've told Harry and he's very happy and crying and on his way and doesn't want her to name the baby Paris. Valerie cries, too, saying she wishes Harry had seen the birth, but is so very happy all her friends are here with her. Doreen makes some crude joke about using her manicure scissors to cut the cord if we hadn't made it to the hospital and frying up the placenta for breakfast.

I look at my watch. Four in the morning. Valerie tells

us that the baby's an Aquarian Wood Dragon, which is not as good as her original plan.

'She'll be neurotic,' Valerie explains with all sincerity.

'Of course she will,' says Doreen.

I tell Valerie the little girl will be what she'll be and that nature and nurture will have influence.

We're all silent for a few moments gazing at Valerie and the baby, then at Valerie again. Then Carron speaks. 'I wouldn't want to go through that all again. Do my life over again. Go through the growing up bit. The puberty bit. The dating bit.'

I tell her she's going to go through the dating bit again soon. 'And you're still growing up, Carron. In fact, you'll probably grow more over the next two years than you have over the past twenty. Bereavement, separation from loved ones, divorce all bring dramatic changes.'

'So does moving house,' Doreen adds.

'Er, yes, but not quite to the same extent as the others,' I say.

'Well, I wouldn't want to live this life again. It's hard,' Carron repeats.

'It is *hard*. But I think that's what they call character building stuff. Makes us what we are.'

'I'm not going to call her Paris,' Valerie interrupts, staring at her baby and clearly wanting to change the subject back to what it should be tonight.

Doctor returns and asks us to leave. We hug Valerie and smile at the baby, who is still resolutely red and puffy but a little less squished looking. We're silent as we walk through the hospital corridors, which is unusual for us. Still a bit dazed about everything, I guess. I don't know what the girls are thinking about, but I'm thinking about soooo many things I can't distinguish what from what.

The taxi ride home is quiet. Daisy and Donald ask us how our friend is when we return. I say fine and happy and baby is a girl and doing well. And Valerie has decided to call her Nelly. And they seem relieved that they won't be charged with manslaughter.

We've got three hours of Disney before returning to the train. We take a ride on the teacups, going round and round gently in circles, eventually boring me to tears, and then to the Indiana Jones ride. We're sent up and down and upside down and juddering this and that way violently, which I love but which makes Fran as sick as a parrot, and I realise that's what it's about. Not Fran being sick as a parrot. But this life thing. It's up to me which ride I go on. How fast I want to go. How many times I go on it. And if I want to leave before my time's up or when the gates close. I've just got to decide when I want to get on and off. And it's all to do with timing in life and I've got to get my timing right.

Chapter Fifteen
The Big Four-O

I wake up at 8:32 to the sound of ELO's 'Mr Blue Skies,' and hey presto, I'm suddenly no longer a thirty-something—what all thirty-nine-year-olds call themselves, while younger thirties are not so ambivalent about specifying their age—I'm forty. And I feel ever so slightly different. I get up and look in the mirror. No, no more wrinkles. Can still do the box splits? Yes, yes, can still do them. And side splits? Yes, they're fine, too. It's weird doing exercises in the nude in front of a mirror, but I suppose that's what I look like to my boyfriends in bed. And Angie for that matter. It's the only time I probably get to see me how they see me when they're having sex with me. And may I say, I don't look all that bad. Not bad at all.

I'll be honest. I thought I would be so cool about

turning forty. It's another birthday after all, like any other, but truth is, it's not. It feels different. Better different. I'm fit, have the attention of a younger man, and a daughter who is leaving home for college, so I am starting a new life. Which sounds good to me. But as I wake up on June fourteenth, the day I was born forty years ago, I feel rather odd. A bit light-headed. A bit other-worldly, out of body almost. Perhaps it's an anxiety attack that I wasn't expecting. Perhaps I will walk outside my front door and people will look at me as an older woman, a middle-aged woman, a woman who is no longer sexy, but more mother earth. Eek. I took in what Doreen said to me about being a mother, about it being the most important role women have in life. And it is important, the most important. But I like my identity. My sexual identity.

I've decided to make it like any other day. I'm working, so at least I'm busy. I will be seeing Joe, though he's got some case in the morning, and I'm having lunch with Fran and Doreen. Valerie is at home with Nelly, who hasn't left her arms, or her nipples, I don't think, since the day she came out of her in Paris, and Carron has been taken away by her new love to Prague and for a short while, anyway, has forgotten her friends in the heat of stomach-churning wonderful lust, not eating, champagne at midnight, do not disturb bedroom signs, all-night foreplay, doing interesting things with strawberries and rediscovering sexy lingerie. Bliss.

We're meeting at Fredericks, in Islington, which is a

lovely restaurant with horrible prices but does a fixed price lunch which is doable on our salaries.

I've dressed in a Jocada outfit that's simple and sexy and feminine. It's something I always feel confident wearing, but I'm just meeting Doreen and Fran, supper with Sarah tonight, so as I walk through the door of Fred's I'm feeling good and I'm cool and feeling fuck!

'Surprise!' Aghhhhhhhh.

What seems like a hundred maniacally smiling faces are grinning from ear to ear and all shouting, screeching, bellowing 'Surprise!' at me. I just go 'aghhhhhh' for what seems like forever, like some virgin who's come violently for the first time and doesn't know what the fuck she's supposed to do with all this energy.

I beam manically back, feeling like a dancer on stage, who's got to smile through the pain. I wanted a quiet lunch with the girls, I've got a full frontal fortieth birthday bash and I've got to be smiley and shiny with everyone, otherwise I look an ungrateful selfish bitch.

I seek out the faces of the Disney girls as I now call them. Valerie's even there without Nelly. Perhaps she's locked her away in a darkened cupboard somewhere, only to emerge when she needs a feed. I can see Doreen, Fran, Carron, yep, all there, and Sarah, who's approaching me with a glass of champagne and a guilty expression.

'Sorry, Mum. Sorry. Know you wanted a quiet Saturday with your teenage daughter who'd promised to cook you a chicken casserole with her own fair hands, with lots of garlic and white wine and soy sauce and TLC. And you'll get that some other time, but today, you've got this instead.'

And she gives me a hug and a glass which I drink straight down like any virgin fortieth birthday girl would do.

Fran's voice echoes over the noise, 'Bet you didn't expect this. Not after the Disney trip, I bet. But Sarah organised it long before we did, so we couldn't really let her in on it. And she thought Disney would be a good idea, too.'

I recognise neighbours, friends I haven't seen for years (God, Janice has put on weight—is she pregnant?), some ex-clients are even here. Brian's here with his partner Orlando (they are sweet. They look camp out of the office but hey ho), my cousins are here—the ones I like, and the ones I don't, but you chose friends not family, don't you. I hug all of them in turn, my Jocando getting gradually more crushed and my hair (I'm so pleased I washed it today—I was thinking of letting it go), more rumpled. I'm offered salmon and what looks like monkfish nibbles but I'm too nervous to swallow. So I hold a salmon bite for a good five minutes before I find a ledge to plop it on without anyone noticing.

My glass is never empty and I'm starting to enjoy this surprise. I'm looking round and thinking it's so good to see all of them. And then I see Joe, smiling at me, in his Paul Smith suit, looking more casual, no tie, a few buttons undone, white linen shirt. He looks simply gorgeous.

He lifts his glass and walks toward me. I feel sixteen

which is good, because for once I feel younger than he looks.

'Happy birthday, Hazel,' he whispers, kissing me on the cheek. And I blush. But I can blame it on the champagne.

'I'm not blushing, you know. It's the champagne.'

'Of course it is.'

My heart is beating so loudly I can hear it go bang bang bang bang, and I'm sure those around me hear it, too, as they turn around and look at me, at us.

I can't stop grinning. I try but it's very difficult because it just comes out like some distorted smirk which feels and must look painful. So I allow myself to be unashamedly and look unashamedly happy in Joe's company. After staring at each other, for a few minutes I manage to say something marginally intelligible.

'This is what my forty years is all about—not the stuff I've accumulated over the years, but the people, the friendships, the loves I've made. Must admit when I saw everybody I thought "oh fuck", but this is sooo good. Sarah is so wonderful doing this for me. Have you been introduced?'

'Not directly. We spoke briefly on the phone.'

'Let me introduce you then.' I turn around and Sarah's right behind me, grinning almost as manically as I was a minute ago.

'Sarah, this is Joe, I work with him. Joe, this is Sarah, my daughter.'

'Lovely to meet you, Sarah. Hazel tells me you're an aspiring politician.'

'Did you, Mum! Oh, no, I'm interested in a lot of things. I'm interested in the law, you meet all the good-looking men in law.'

I stare at my daughter. She's flirting with my man. She's making doe eyes at him. Okay, he's not my man. We're not going out or anything, but we like each other. This is so weird. For the first time in my life I think I feel a little jealous of my daughter. I've never wanted to be young again, who in their right mind would want puberty all over again (I don't think I'm fully out of it sometimes), but she looks stunning today, and he looks gorgeous and they would make a nice couple. This is so weird. I don't think I've even dealt with a case where a man's gone off with the stepdaughter or his own for that matter, but I'm sure it happens. Oh, get real, Hazel, keep the thought out of your head. This is silly. But could I seriously go out with someone, develop a relationship with a man whom my daughter was attracted to in that way? I'd never thought of that as a problem. Well, I had, but never realistically. Work issues, yes, age, possibly, but daughter fancying my boyfriend, or potential boyfriend—how the fuck do I deal with that?

Joe replies, 'I know. I entered it because there were so many gorgeous-looking women in it. Your mum for one. She's a stunner, don't you think?'

I'm a bit taken back. Joe has just called me a stunner. He's never complimented me in or out of the office. I know he thinks me efficient, and know he likes me, and can't get me out of his head and all that, but he's never complimented me, and he's chosen to do it for the first time in front of Sarah, who's obviously got a crush on him. This is so bizarre I want to laugh. I feel like pushing her out of the way, as though we're in some playground and I want Joe to kiss me first.

'Yes, my mum is gorgeous, that's where I get my good looks from I'm told.'

Hussy. My daughter is a hussy. I smile and say nothing.

'You do indeed,' Joe says, looking at me, into my eyes and at my lips which makes me want to melt on the spot because I've drunk more than I did at the Paella and haven't eaten anything and am feeling extremely horny and competitive. Oh, Hazel—this is your daughter, this is Sarah. This is Sarah. Chill. She is more important than any man. She has always been more important than any man. But she has also never fancied any of the men I've been with, because they've been old enough to be her father. And Joe isn't. He's midway. And it's more socially acceptable for the older man and younger woman than it is the older woman and younger man.

Joe smiles, I think realising Sarah has a crush on him, but our conversation is stopped by a very drunk Brian who gives me a big bear hug and tells me I look amazing and why don't I wear things like this in the office.

'Why don't you wear things like this in the office, Hazel? We'd get a lot more business.'

I regain composure and turn to him, still a bit red in the face.

'It depends what sort of business you want to get,' I say, trying not to slur.

I turn back to find Joe and Sarah deep in conversation. I've lost my boyfriend even before I've got to first base. To my daughter of all people, and he's still only just out of a relationship. She's beautiful and I can't deprive her of happiness and he's nice. Fuck, I know he's nice— I fancy him. He would provide for her well and he's a good person with principles. Hazel, you can be cool about this. You can be cool. Then why the fuck don't I feel cool. I feel upset. I feel ridiculous. And I know it's just the drink. It's got to be just the drink. I must find one of the girls before I do or say something absurd, or worse, hurtful. Where's Doreen, Valerie, Fran, Carron? Where are they? I turn around and find them all staring at me from afar.

'So what are you looking at?' I shout, walking up to them as naturally as I possibly can.

'You,' replies Doreen. 'We were thinking of giving you the bumps, but it seems a bit unfair, since Joe is here. That's him, isn't it?' she says nodding in his direction. I turn round. He's still deep in conversation with hussy daughter (only joking, only joking).

'He's very nice. He doesn't look his age. Seems older than that. About midthirties I would guess,' offers Carron. 'Very nice. Nice eyes. Like his dress sense.'

'Yes, I like it, too,' I say, turning away from the happy (shit, shit, bugger shit) couple. In my head I imagine being mother of the bride. Stop it, stop it, Hazel. This is depressing. Get another image in your head. The dirty dancing. Yes, that's better.

'So have you kissed him yet?' asks Fran.

'No, not yet. He's giving himself space, which is a good thing, after such a long relationship. He needs to.'

'What harm would a kiss do?'

'None.'

'So get in there, girl. It's your birthday.'

Bolstered by my bullish friends I turn to find Sarah behind me, minus Joe.

'So many could make it, Mum, and I asked everyone I thought you'd like to be here. Didn't realise you were working with such a tasty guy. Joe's gorgeous. Absolute hunk. Why didn't you tell me about him?'

'Yes, he is gorgeous, isn't he. Good solicitor, too.'

'Must admit when I saw him I thought, for an older man I quite fancied him, but do you know what? I think he's got the hots for you. Bet you didn't know that. I know what you're like. Very tunnel visioned sometimes. But he kept asking me if you have any boyfriends and thought you were gorgeous and it was so distracting having someone as beautiful as you in the office. Very complimentary he was. Gorgeous, but bit old for me. Bit old.'

My daughter is no longer a hussy. And I feel utterly, utterly ashamed. Bad, horrible, wretched mother that I am. I was jealous of my daughter. Of her happiness. But I'm so relieved.

'Bit old. How old does that make me?' I laugh.

'Old enough to be my mum. And I think he likes you.'

'I think he likes you, too,' chips in Doreen who's heard everything.

'So do I, so do I, so do I,' echo the rest of the girls.

I'm in the playground again. I feel as though I'm in the school playground and I'm having fun and playing kiss chase with one of the boys but I've got to chase him. No, I've got to allow myself to be caught.

Chapter Sixteen
Lump

Seven the following morning, having had a fabulous birthday party, but still managed not to get a birthday kiss (except peck on the cheek which doesn't count) from Joe. I get a phone call. It's Doreen.

A lump. Doreen has found a lump in her left breast. She thinks it's nothing serious, but is having it examined.

'A lump. Yes, a lump. Was just checking as you do occasionally, when something's a bit sore or the bra doesn't fit quite right. Good thing I did it really.'

'Oh, hell, Doreen, have you seen a doctor?'

'Yes, of course I have, Hazel. Problem is, it's bigger than a pea. It's about the size of a golf ball. Not nice. I don't have big tits but, well, I haven't told Mick. Not yet anyway. He couldn't cope with knowing this.'

I'm stunned. The balloon has popped and I feel sick.

This doesn't happen to people I know. This happens to people on TV, in films, in books, but not people I know. And not to Doreen. To someone weak and feeble and a bit of a nonentity who doesn't have any fight in them and will just curl up and die, perhaps. But not Doreen. She's a fighter and funny and sexy and strong and lumps don't get in her way. She's worried and I want to cry. I don't. I just ask if I can be there at the hospital or help out at home at all.

'Oh no, God no, Jane at work is being wonderful. I've told her stuff and she cried a lot, bless her, but she's being wonderful. And Mick, well, Mick's Mick and I've fudged it a bit as, well, as I don't want to see his reaction. It won't help me. I know he's got a right to know, but it won't help me.'

'He should know, Doreen,' I say, 'he should know.'

'I'll tell him if it gets really serious.'

'It sounds really serious already.'

'No, no, we don't know that yet. Not for sure. No need worrying him needlessly. And if there is something to worry about, then he'll know he'll have something to worry about rather that worrying about if he should be worried or not. No need worrying him needlessly because it doubles my stress rather than lessens it because he can't handle the stress so I have to handle him being stressed as well as my stress if you see what I mean.'

Doreen is gabbling. She is stressed.

'Well, I can handle the stress, Doreen. I can handle the stress. So what have you done about it?'

'Been to the doctors. The doctor says it's malignant, which obviously means the Big C. It's strange when they say *cancer*. You expect them to say it in a whisper as though it's a rude word, like *fuck*, but they don't, they say it in a very matter-of-fact way, like *book*, or *dog*, or *handbag*. And I was a bit stunned when he told me because I thought it was a cyst and they've run in my family, so I thought it would be that. But it wasn't. And he told me as I was on private that I could have it done immediately, which I obviously am. And I was due to have it today, but can't because I'm working today and there's an important conference call I've got to take, so it's on Friday.'

I'm so angry.

'What do you mean you were due to have the operation today and you're not because you're working? For Christ's sake, Doreen, I don't want you here, I want you in hospital. I want you here for many years to come, not today.'

'Oh, Hazel, I am going in and I will be fine. Absolutely fine.'

'Have you told anyone else?'

'Only Jane and you, now. I haven't told the other girls yet. I don't want to rain on Fran's parade. The girl's getting married soon. And Carron has her own issues and Valerie's wrapped up in little Nelly.'

'I'm coming to the hospital with you on Friday.'

'Don't be so ridiculous.'

'No, I'm coming. You need some support for this. Even if you can't tell Mick. You've been with me through my tough times. You were there through my divorce, sitting at the bottom of the stairs with me.'

'Yes, I believe I told you to cut his balls off.'

'Yes, well, perhaps that wasn't your most constructive piece of advice ever.'

'It would have worked, though.'

'Doubtless it would, but I'm not talking about me, I'm talking about you. I'm going to round up the girls. You need to tell them. They are your friends, Doreen. We can help.'

Chapter Seventeen
Confronting Fiona

Knock on the door.

I'm in the house with the girls. I've organised a light lunch round my place—for Doreen and the girls. Just nibbles and wine and stuff. They all know now. About the lump. About it being malignant. And hopefully it being caught in time. Because most are, aren't they. That's what we all think and say and say to Doreen, when we talk about it. Not that we want to make it the main point of conversation at the moment. Not at the moment. So it's just me and the girls. Fran and I are going to the hospital with Doreen this week. She's having her operation to have her breast removed. We're going to give her support. Everyone is tense but trying to be very cool. We're going to the hospital because we want to. And because she's asked us. But she seems in good spirits. She's talking about sex and boardroom politics and the guy at the gym with the cute arse as though she hasn't a care in the world.

I open the door. A slim brown-haired girl with pretty eyes is staring at me. I have met this girl once before. Only once. She came into my office a month ago. Just to say hi to her boyfriend. Who at the time was Joe. At the time. Fiona is not smiling. I feign that I can't remember her. Or that she was once Joe's girlfriend. I check her hands for knives. But can't see any. She's with a friend, who's taller and plumper than her and looks angrier than her. Fiona knows where I live. Play cool.

'Hello.' Her voice trembles slightly.

'Hello, Fiona isn't it?'

'I understand you and Joe are seeing each other.'

I look at her. Her eyes are puffy and red. She looks tired. Not as tired as Doreen, but tired.

'We're not seeing each other, Fiona. We work together.'

'I know what's going on and I don't know how you could do it.'

I can hear her voice breaking. I'm embarrassed for her. I don't want her to carry on because I've been in her shoes. I wouldn't do what she's doing. I would have too much pride. But I feel for her. I resist the urge to mother her, just in case she has a knife hidden somewhere.

'Have you spoken to Joe?'

'Yes.'

'What did he say?'

'That he more than likes you.'

Joe has told Fiona he more than likes me. I'm confused

and rather cross. I don't want to tell Fiona that Joe hasn't told me he was going to tell her, or get into the nitty gritty of non-kiss, dirty dancing, because then that will cause unnecessary hurt, and because, damn it, I more than like him, too. But Joe, how can a man be so lucid in court and so bloody inept out of it? So I speak.

'Right, well, that's between Joe and I. If you have an issue with Joe, you should speak to Joe. Not to me.'

'I'm asking you to leave him alone.'

'It's his decision, Fiona.'

I feel quite sick. I felt sick because of Doreen and her situation and now I feel even more sick. I may just throw up on the doorstep right in front of her. I remember David's girlfriend saying this to me over the phone when I confronted her with their affair and this is what she said. *It's David's decision*. And I freeze, because I'm now the other woman. Okay, I haven't split up a marriage where there is a child involved, but I've caused pain, this I can see on her face. This face that was so much happier when I first saw it. Fuck, double fuck, fuck. Why can't she be nasty and angry? Much easier to come back against.

'It's also your decision.'

Christ, does everything go round in circles? This is just what I said to David's girlfriend. That is exactly what I said. *It's also your decision,* I said to her. And then I said to her, *That is all I need to know about you.* And hung up. Mind you, she turned out to be a neurotic, moody, incredibly arrogant cow who in the end made David's life hell, so what do I care.

'I think you should speak to Joe about this. This is none of my business. If you want to resolve it with him, you do it, but it's none of my business.'

'Have you kissed him?' she asks. I can tell she's praying for a *no*. She wants a *no*. Her whole demeanour tells me she wants me to say no so she can live the lie. She wants me to say we've just had tea together. I remember this is what I desperately wanted David's girlfriend to say. Fat chance. If I say any more she will continue the conversation and I don't want her to, for her sake as much as mine. So I say, 'I'm with my friends, and this is not a good time.'

Fiona takes a breath. 'All I want to say is, I couldn't do what you have done. I couldn't have stooped so low. I couldn't have stolen someone else's boyfriend. You could have any man you wanted and you took Joe. You took someone else's love. I hope you're pleased with yourself.'

Fiona leaves in tears. The best friend still scowling. I check for knives. No, still no knives. I can feel best friend is mouthing 'I'll be back' like some Arnold Schwarzenegger clone.

I return to the girls who are staring at me. They've heard everything. I expect catcalls of bitch and slut. Instead Carron says, 'You handled that with grace and dignity and sensitivity.'

I hadn't expected that from Carron.

Fran remarks, 'You did. You could have been meaner or less honest, but you were sympathetic without being a pushover.'

'So you're not judging me?' I say.

'Friends don't judge,' adds Doreen matter-of-factly. 'You said so yourself. Friends don't put friends in little boxes. We like you for who you are, faults and all. Plus the fact you can get a man ten years your junior from a girl who looks like that, well, to be honest, you've made us all feel fucking good about turning forty. For fuck's sake, you've had a girl looking that stunning telling you that you could get any man you want.'

'You didn't answer her but you can tell us, have you slept with him?' Doreen asks.

'No, I haven't. Strange that, isn't it. But, well, it's quite exciting. Seeing each other every day, most days, and just waiting. He still needs time by himself, because of Fiona. I don't know why he's told her, because, well, he hasn't told me. But strangely enough, we haven't done anything.'

Doreen looks bemused. I don't think she understands the concept of trying to get to know someone emotionally before you see them naked. I'll be the first to admit I'm usually impatient for the first kiss and sexual encounter, mainly because I feel silly trying to play coy about what I want and don't want. And also, to be blunt, because I love having sex. I've never been one of these women that prefers chocolate to sex, even bad sex. But then I'm much more fussy about my sex than I am about my chocolate. Being sexually innocent in your early twenties is provocative, being sexually innocent as you turn forty is just plain sad. However, I'm finding the fact Joe and I haven't made love after all these months intensifies the electricity.

Four bottles of Chardonnay later, Waitrose nibbles, and peppermint teas, we are all emotionally exhausted and hoarse with philosophising about life, boob jobs and younger men.

The girls leave together. Fiona and best friend are not waiting with knives but the others come out with me just in case. To bear witness should I get stabbed.

Chapter Eighteen
Meeting Joe's Parents

I understand.

Joe understands that the weekend he has organised for us in Verona, to be our first romantic time together since his split from Fiona has to be cancelled. He looks for a split second disappointed, but he understands. I resent the disappointment. Understand it, but resent it. Doreen is more important. But I see it in his eyes he understands. He says there will be a next time. And I say I hope so but that Doreen needs me now and I want her to have next times. And I want her to have a forty-first and forty-second and forty-third year that are good and wonderful. And I'm selfish, so I want her company. And I want her to spend some of her next times with me. I don't want to lose her to a heaven that may not appreciate her the way I do. The way her friends do. I know she can be bossy and very abrupt and rude, but I've known her since I was eleven, I know she cares about all of us, and I love her dearly. I love her irreverence, her take-life-by-the-balls attitude, her drink from the cup and nick someone else's and drink theirs, too, if they're too stupid or lazy to do it. I love the way she defends her friends and family and yet isn't averse to stripping us down a peg or two. I love the way when I meet her she greets me with an open warm smile and makes me laugh within the first few minutes, and gasp the next. I love the way I am when I'm with her.

But today, after work, I'm meeting Joe's parents. Sheila and Norman Ryan. They're not Australian, they just have Australian names. They've been married for over thirty years. Norman was a tennis player and deputy headmaster, who was in the army in India. He met Sheila when he was at a dance. It was an 'excuse me,' and Norman was dancing with another woman and Sheila excused the dance (very forward at the time because only men were supposed to do it) and she danced with him and the rest led to marriage and babies. In that order.

They live in a house in Richmond, so only a stone's throw from me in Wimbledon village. They're on the hill in a home they couldn't afford if it were up for sale now. Fine for them. And they have a garden and a view of the river. And take walks along the green and occasionally meet the Attenboroughs (David and Richard) who are on nodding terms with them, if not buddy-buddy. All this I hear in the car on the way to Joe's parents. He talks about them with an open affection. He doesn't come across as a mummy's or daddy's boy. More someone who has been loved and nurtured by both of them. I'm looking forward to meeting them.

I want to make a good impression so I've spent an hour prior in the bathroom trying to make myself look beautiful, and okay, I admit it, younger.

I'm still upstairs de-ageing my face when he knocks on our door. I'm trying to puff out those lines round my eyes. The Dermologica package says it will 'kill the wrinkles round the eye area.' It contains Vitamin E, Vitamin C and Provitamin B5 and licorice, comfrey and burdock. Am I supposed to put this on my face or eat it? But the lines are still there. I can still see the lines. Lots of the little fucking things. And they are not disappearing. They are still there. I can see them. I don't need a microscope. And they're not laughter lines, they're I'm-getting-older lines. And I'm getting facial hairs. Lots of them. I've got a definite moustache. Okay, it's only light and white and fluffy but it's definitely there. It could turn into a hard brittle one and then Joe will get chin burn like I did when I went out with Simon that time and he was such a passionate kisser but I had this big horrible scab on my chin for weeks. Everyone thought I had scabies, whatever that is.

I'm ready. I check myself out in the mirror. I look okay. I'm wearing pink. I look good in pink. Can a woman turning forty still wear pink? Not if she looks forty. But what does a forty-year-old look like these days? Everyone is looking better, fitter, younger. So I look good for my age because I don't look my age, so is age a moot point? Oh, shut up, mind. Shut up. Shut up. Just look in the mirror, Hazel, and look at yourself and tell me what you see. I see a woman wearing pink who is glowing with happiness and nerves and anticipation and feels like a teenager meeting her boyfriend's parents for the first time. But it's the real first time, because I've never felt quite this excited before. Not even when I met David's parents, mainly because they were so under-whelmed with meeting me. Of course, Joe's may be the same. Perhaps it's me and parents. But this time I want to impress, but I want to be me. And if I'm myself I think they'll like me.

I walk down stairs. Joe's wearing all black and looks edible. The only way to describe him is edible. He looks at me as though he wants to eat me, too. Perhaps this is not a good look to nurture in front of my daughter or his parents. I go toward him and kiss him on both cheeks and then notice Sarah, who is grinning from ear to ear. Sarah shakes hands and asks if he wants something to drink. I say we've got to go, Joe says we have time and he would love to. I think, shit, this leaves time for Sarah to make immediate spontaneous decision about whether she hates or just loathes him, and is this wise.

I leave them in the kitchen chatting. It's best to leave them by themselves. They're still talking half an hour later so I walk in.

Sarah looks up and smiles at me. 'Hi, Mum, I've got to

go now. Joe was telling me how he knows about the college I'll be at. He says the music scene is very good there.'

'Really?'

'Yeah, anyway, have a lovely time. Good to see you again, Joe.'

She gets up, and says, 'Have fun.'

And I look at her and think she means it. I think she likes him. I think she likes him. But not that way.

Quickly, she kisses me on the cheek and whispers, 'I like him.'

The journey to Richmond takes less than ten minutes, despite the fact that traffic in this pretty part of just out of London suburb is usually dreadful. He tells me I look beautiful and strokes my cheek. I just want to look young.

Two people stand in the doorway of a large Victorian house fronted with large pink and yellow hydrangeas. They look in their late fifties but Joe assures me both his parents are in their seventies and eighties, his father being ten years older than his mother. They smile. The man's whole face beams. The woman's smile is on her lips. To be expected as I'm dating her little boy. I try not to fall over or trip up as I walk along their pathway, as they're able to stand for a good few seconds before I'm able to shake hands and introduce myself. I feel about sixteen. They ignore my hand and give me a hug each which I find rather sweet.

I get shown to the sitting room, which is immaculate but in a comfortable sort of way. Creams and browns and some greens and navy everywhere, with watercolours of boats. Some pictures I recognise of Tuscany and Florence and Siena, probably painted by local artists. I get the 'Joe has told us a lot about you. Lovely to meet you. So I believe you live near here. Oh yes, but sorry we took such a long time getting here' chatter.

Cups of tea and battenburg cake (I didn't know they still made that) with bread pudding (made by Sheila) are put out, and tinned salmon sandwiches with cucumber. The Ritz couldn't have done better. Norman tells me about his time in India and how he was given the toilets to clean and put so much water over them, none of the soldiers bothered to use them. Sheila tells me how when Joe was born, Norman was playing tennis for the county, and won that day. He was playing doubles with his partner Norman Booth, and it was quoted in the local newspaper. Norman Ryan won the Richmond Cup today with Norman Booth spurred on by the birth of son Joe who was born as the last game was played. Sheila shows me the newspaper cutting which she presents with pride. They ask about Sarah, who I explain is off to college this year, to become, hopefully a journalist or barrister or actor, she can't work out which. They talk about Joe in an affectionate but not cloying way and they make me feel, like, well, like one of the family. Sheila tells me some stories about Joe as a little boy while we eat supper, lasagne cooked to perfection, and the most alcoholic sherry trifle I've ever eaten (and enjoyed). They're funny and fun, warm and unpretentious and I'm not surprised they've produced a son like Joe. Doesn't always follow, it's just nice to know it does sometimes.

As I'm sitting there with tea and cake, talking to his dad about tennis and tennis knee and how they have much better cartilage operations these days, and to his mum about being an only child, and do I ever miss having brothers and sisters—and I say no, because I never had any, so don't know what I'm missing, I think of my own parents. And how much I miss them. And how much I wish I could have introduced Joe to them. I wonder how he would have been. How he would have reacted to my mum's faux pas and my dad's dry sense of humour. I think he would have liked my dad. I think he would. I can hear my dad whispering to me now. I can sense he's smiling at me, and laughing. I think about my dad as I'm listening to Norman talk about Joe as a little boy. I can feel his arms around me, holding me tight as he did when I was a girl. Like when I used to watch *Doctor Who* when I was little and I would hide underneath his jumper and watch through the holes at the Daleks and the Cybermen and that episode where the shop mannequin dolls came alive and walk out of the shop window and kill people with their plastic grip. And Mum would come into the sitting room and complain that I was stretching Dad's jumper and Dad would look up and tell her it didn't matter, and she would say it did, because she had to wash the bloody thing. And I would stay underneath the jumper, snuggling up, safe from the Daleks being destroyed by Jon Pertwee, who always was the best, most effective Doctor Who in my opinion. If Mum and Dad were alive they'd be over eighty now. My mother would have probably become more neurotic and my father more browbeaten but still the kind gentle soul I remember. He would always say to me, 'Be patient with your mother, Hazel, be patient. She says stupid things, but she loves you. Remember, if you can't say something good about someone, don't say anything at all'. My dad would have made a lousy divorce lawyer.

As we leave, as the sun is setting, Sheila tells me it was lovely to meet me (I hope it was) and Norman hugs me and tells me that he hopes we meet soon.

'I'm not as good a cook as Sheila unfortunately.'

'Don't worry, we'll eat anything, within reason, and if it's really bad, we'll bring our own.'

I think he would have got on well with my dad. And may even have charmed my mother into silence. Well, perhaps not silence. Perhaps gentle banter.

'Do you think they like me?' I whisper to Joe after five minutes silence in the car.

'Of course. Mum even thought you looked much younger than forty. She said you reminded her of herself when she was younger.'

'Is that a good thing?'

'I think so. Only she was worried Dad might fancy you, too.'

Joe looks at me and smiles. I know he's joking this time. 'They also said they would love to meet again, so if you do want to invite them around, they'll be happy to come.'

'So they don't mind their little boy going out with an older woman then?'

'Oh, no, Mum actually said she wished she'd done it. Not in front of my dad of course. It's just that women age more slowly than men. The age difference isn't so much when you're in your twenties, thirties, forties, fifties or even sixties. But when you get older the ten-year gap means more. You become a carer, which Mum is becoming. I don't somehow think I'll be looking after you. It will be the other way round.'

'So you don't see yourself with a younger woman?'

'Younger women irritate me, Hazel. I have nothing in common with them. And anyway, what would I want with one when I have an older one with the body of someone ten years her junior.'

Joe's still saying the right thing, at the right time, in the right way. That evening, after Joe drops me off, giving me a long, passionate snog on my doorstep, (no groping, which is so rare and romantic these days—plus he knows I've got to be there for Doreen the next day) I call Fran.

'How are you, darling?' she asks.

'Oh fine, just met Joe's parents.'

'Nice?'

'Wonderful. But you don't like someone for their parents, do you?'

'It helps. I don't particularly like Daniel's, but he's worth it. Worth the hassle.'

I notice Fran's a bit down. Her voice sounds slightly lower and she's talking more slowly.

'Are you okay?'

'Oh yes, fine, still having last-minute doubts. Could we

meet? I've got something to tell you. Something I want to discuss.'

'Can't it wait till tomorrow, when we go to see Doreen?'

'Not really. It's just that, well, I'm pregnant.'

'Well done.'

'Yep. Only problem is, it's not Daniel's.'

Chapter Nineteen
Fran's Last Year of Being Single

Fran is surprising me. She's on the phone at one in the morning. She's pregnant with another man's baby one month before she's due to be married to Daniel. The man she's cherished for nearly ten years. She's waited for this moment and she's got pregnant by another man. It's not the sort of discussion you should have over the phone with a best friend. We're with Doreen tomorrow and, well, that's enough stress for all of us for the next ten years, not just the next twelve months.

My mind is full of so many questions. Whose is it, what's she going to do about it, how did she find time, does she love him, does Daniel know, does she love Daniel, is she going through with the wedding, does anyone else know, is she going to have the baby, how does she feel, does she want a hug, does she know of a clinic? I know Fran has thought of all those questions and probably the answers as well and she will tell me in her own time. She does.

'Hazel, I met Paul six months ago at work. There was a physical attraction, but I obviously didn't pursue it because, well, I'm getting married and he knew it. But we had lunch and tea and coffee after work, that sort of thing, and we made each other laugh. It was fun, and a bit like Daniel and I were at the beginning of our relationship. But it's not like that anymore. We've grown apart. And the irony is, we're getting married *and* we've grown apart.'

I say nothing. I just listen. She expects me to speak, but when I don't, she continues.

'I had sex with him a few months ago, just before you went in for the Brazilian but I didn't want to tell you then. I wanted to, but couldn't. I just felt it was last-minute nerves and if anything happened it would be like the last fling. And I'm sensible. Everyone says I'm sensible and I don't do this sort of thing. You know, behave irresponsibly. But do you know, I wanted to. I'm almost forty and I wanted to do something mad and bad and, well, dangerous, and be wild and adventurous, which I've never been in my life. Never been allowed to be and this was it. So I went away with Paul. For a weekend to Le Manoir, Raymond Blanc's place. We had the Provence Room, very romantic and lots of eating in the room, and off each other, and I was terrified we would be found out but it made the moments even more intense and exciting. Paul's lovely and I think it's just lust, not love, but we do have a chemistry. And he's just divorced himself and likes me, but it may have been a rebound thing, so I'm not sure, but it's been good so far. You know, what you feel for Joe, I feel for Paul. That buzz. And I don't feel that for Daniel anymore, but I know that doesn't last. Does it?'

She doesn't wait for me to answer. I think it's rhetorical anyway.

'Paul knows it was only a passing thing, but we've become involved and he doesn't think I'm being honest with myself and I don't either, but I've got to go through with it. But I can't have an abortion yet, I've got to wait until it's twelve weeks. And, well, I'm on honeymoon then. Honeymoon. So do I just have the baby and pretend it's Daniel's, because I don't want to abort, or do I come clean with him and admit to the affair and the baby and go our separate ways? I can't talk to my parents or his parents. And I'm not ready for marriage to Daniel. I don't feel ready for marriage. I may be forty, but I'm not ready. Some women are in their twenties, but I don't think I will ever be. And Daniel is wonderful if a bit conventional and I'm not the woman he first met and I'd make him very unhappy.'

Slight pause for breath.

'So what do you think I should do?'

There are some women you expect in life to behave irrationally. There are others you think will never, ever behave in any way that is irresponsible. Fran is one of them. She is as black and white as they come. She is the

I dotter and T crosser to end all anal but loveable people. I'm gobsmacked and anxious for her at the same time. She hasn't been able to share and talk to anyone about this and it would have helped perhaps if she could have done. If she could have spoken to us at Le Pont, or when we went to EuroDisney, or me, at the health club. I'm her best friend and she couldn't talk to me. But then again, neither could Doreen tell us about the lump. What is it with my friends? I think we can share everything and find out they all have secrets they keep to themselves until it is too late. Until they realise they can't handle it alone and they need help. They need help.

'And I wanted to tell you at your birthday, I felt I could and then Doreen told you about her lump and it wasn't appropriate. And I wanted to tell you about the baby at EuroDisney but then Valerie had her baby and then there was Le Pont but Carron was sobbing and it wasn't right. The timing wasn't right. My timing isn't right.'

At least I feel I'm not the only one who gets her timing wrong sometimes.

'Are you still there?'

I haven't said anything and Fran is asking me if I'm still there.

'Yes. I'm still here. Fran, how can I help?'

'How can you help? I've balanced what I should do. I've balanced what I should do, do my duty, and I've balanced what I should do, for Fran, for me.'

'And what should you do for you? What do you want to do?'

'For the day, for the moment, I should go through with the wedding, because that is what everyone expects and I will go down that aisle and be a good wife to Daniel and love him and be faithful to him and have a quickie abortion when I return from honeymoon. That is what I will do. I will not see Paul again. He doesn't know about the baby and that's for the best. That is what I should do.'

Fran does not say this with conviction.

'You are not saying this with conviction, Fran. I'm not convinced this is what you want to do.'

'What I want to do. What mad Fran wants to do, is to have the baby, cancel the wedding and run off with Paul and take a risk. I want to go for it and have the baby and do it with grace. But Daniel wouldn't understand and my family would disown me and if I felt I made a mistake I could never go back on this. And Daniel would never forgive me and I would lose a friend and he wouldn't understand, would he? He wouldn't understand. And then it would be nasty and he would get nasty. And I know you've always thought he's wet and a bit of a drip, but he's got a dark side and he'd get nasty.'

I listen to Fran.

'Do you want to marry a man with a dark side who would get nasty? If he loves you, he will be upset but he will let you go. It's a lot to ask of a man to forgive you, but it's more to ask of him to marry you and then tell him later on, perhaps even on your honeymoon when you've had too much to drink and are overridden with guilt, that you have someone else's baby and you're not sure you've done the right thing and you may do that.'

'Never.'

'Why not? I did something similar. Women all over the world, Fran, walk down that aisle and are totally unsure they are doing the right thing. I get hundreds of clients say the same thing—both men and women.'

'It's just something to cover their own back because they feel a failure. That their life has been a failure.'

'I agree. But they went through with it. They did what they thought was the right thing and they lived to regret it. Not all of it perhaps, not having the children bit, but they lived to regret the other bit. And when you walk down that aisle, Fran, you should be a hundred percent sure you are doing the right thing.'

'Can anyone be a hundred percent sure of anything?'

'When you get married, yes. When you get married.'

I can sense Fran is silently crying.

'Do you want the baby?'

'I would like the baby, it may be the last opportunity I have to have a baby. I know what trouble and pain Valerie went through to have Nelly. I would like this baby. Paul is a good man. I have money. I could bring it up myself.'

'Bringing up a baby by yourself is not easy, even when you have money.'

'I know, but I want this baby and I can't ask Daniel to support me and I can't lie to Daniel about the baby being his.'

'Hate to ask, but don't you use contraception?'

'I do, but, well, it didn't work. Condom broke.'

'Right, so it was heat of the moment passion.'

'Quite.'

'Worth it?'

'I don't know. We'll see, won't we.'

'So you don't want an abortion. You don't want to marry Daniel and you don't necessarily want to be with the father.'

'Correct.'

'Then you've made your decision.'

'But is it the right one?'

'It's the right one for you, Fran. I will support you in anything you do. As will your friends. Just wish you'd told me before.'

'I know, but we've all got a lot on our plates.'

'I know, but we're friends and if you can't talk to friends who can you talk to?'

'I couldn't tell my parents.'

'I know.'

'I couldn't tell Daniel.'

'I know. Thank you for telling me.'

Silence again. Then Fran says, 'I'll see you tomorrow at the hospital with Doreen. Don't mention anything to her.'

'I won't if you don't want me to, but I think she'd like her mind taken off her own problems and think this will distract her. Certainly distracted me.'

'Distracted you from what?'

'Oh, how Joe's parents were lovely. Made me feel part

of the family and I felt, well, very loved up and safe and, well, happy.'

'What's wrong with that?'

'Because I don't like feeling too happy. I always think nature has a way of balancing things out and something bad is round the corner.'

'Like this.'

'No, this is not bad. Perhaps the timing was good, Fran, and it's a sign telling you not to marry. That your life is beginning like Valerie's is, with a new baby and that's what it's all about. Sometimes things don't go to plan and that's what makes life fun and exciting and dangerous and unexpected and we're old and strong enough now to deal with the curve balls that we couldn't when we were in our twenties.'

'You think so?'

'I know so.'

'Will you be there when I have the baby?'

'Of course. I will also be there if you need some support to tell Daniel and cancel arrangements. I won't ask how he will react.'

'Badly, but that's to be expected.'

'How about Paul?'

'He has three children already but I don't know.'

'Why couldn't you wait to have Daniel's?'

'I don't want Daniel's, Hazel. How can I want Daniel's if I've done something like this to him?'

'What have you done to him? You're not married to him.'

'I've been unfaithful.'

'You've been unfaithful because you were unhappy. Because you are unhappy. Was this an aberration?'

'Well, no.'

'Well, then, you've saved him and saved yourself. And as your maid of honour I'm telling you to not go down that aisle.'

'But all the guests, what do I tell them?'

'I will help you tell them. That you've called it off. Not postponed it. Called it off. Then you're not clock-watching for the next round. And be straight, or as straight as you can be with Daniel. Say you're unhappy and can't marry him and say you're sorry but that's how you feel and see what he says. Listen to what he says.'

'I will. Love you, Hazel.'

'Love you, too.'

I put the phone down. My hands are shaking. They're shaking because this is such a weird conversation and a weird day and I wish, how I wish someone had had that conversation with me before I married David, but then I wouldn't have had Sarah. So perhaps everything happens for a reason. And that's all I can think about Fran. That this has happened for a reason.

Chapter Twenty
Foreplay

Rip.

Sunday morning at GoForIt and Angie's going for it on the under arms and half leg today. As well as the arrow, which I've grown quite fond of over the past few months. I'm updating her on my life.

'Has he seen it yet?' she asks.

'Has who seen what yet?'

'Has your new man seen the arrow?'

'No, Angie. No. We haven't had sex, though I think I'm falling in love with someone I haven't made love to. It's been some time since Joe parted with his girlfriend, but we still haven't made love. I know it's weird.'

'I don't think it's weird. Perhaps a little unconventional, but think it's rather charming actually. Now legs apart.'

I do as Angie says.

'I've never done it this way before. It's always been sex as starters, main course and dessert, but at the age of forty, I'm now finding the excitement in the anticipation. The anticipation of getting naked, of liking and falling in love with someone before making love. My time with Joe—at work and out of it—is one long foreplay. It's been a strangely nonsexual foreplay. Which is unusual for me, because I'm a sexual being.'

'Some women aren't into sex, Hazel. But I know from what you tell me, you like it.'

'I do, but I think stuff's that's been happening to my friends (I think of Fran's bump and Doreen's lump) has made me more aware of what's important to me, has made me become aware of my own body—and things—like sex—have just been pushed aside.'

'Hasn't there been the opportunity then? I suppose you're so busy with work stuff?'

'Oh, there's been opportunity. You can make time, can't you, if you really want to. Yes, we've had lunches and drinks and laughs and held hands, but work and time hasn't allowed sex. Okay, we could have booked into a hotel at lunchtime and had sex or he could have easily slept with me one evening, but to be honest, I haven't allowed it. I want to get to know him first. Doesn't that sound naff?'

'Not at all,' says Angie, tweezing my left armpit for strays.

'But that's how I feel and I'm going with my head, as well as my heart, on this one.'

'Has he pushed for sex?'

'No, he hasn't pushed for sex. He knows I've been preoccupied with my friends. Because my time with them is precious. I'm worried about two friends in particular, who are both going through horrendous times…'

I think, I usually tell Angie everything but what's happening to Doreen and Fran is too raw to talk about, even to her. Doreen's operation wasn't completely successful, as in, wasn't successful. So she's having to go in again and have her breasts removed. She laughs when she talks about it to me over the phone in the early hours, saying she never thought she'd have a boob job, but she's ended up having two. Then Fran. Who told Daniel she wanted to call off the wedding and he got vicious when he found out about the baby. So I've been on the phone at night a lot listening to two of my closest friends sobbing their hearts out and laughing as well. Joe knows I have given them more time than him because they need it. I've given Sarah more time than him because she'll be off soon and this time with her is so very special. Those last few months. Everything has become so intense recently. It's as though each second of life, of happiness, is a tangible gift that I've got to appreciate and soak in, because it just won't be there forever. He hasn't been selfish and forced himself on me. He's stood back and been gently supportive. And he's probably still mourning for his girlfriend. So he's giving me and giving himself space. Angie appears oblivious that I'm deep in thought.

'No worries, darling. How's it been at work with this guy?'

'We've been very professional at work, but occasionally Joe comes into the office, under the pretext of discussing some case or another, sits me on my desk, his arms around me, and I feel wonderful. Not controlled by him. Or controlling him. Just enjoying the moment with him. Not competing for power or being threatened by him. I love the way he keeps his eyes open when he kisses me. I love the way he strokes my back when he's kissing me. I love the way he holds me not too tight and not too lightly. I love the way he's taller than me. And broader than me. And secure in himself. I love so many things about him. But can I love him?'

I sit up as Angie puts the finishing touches to my right half leg.

'*How can you love him?* Just love him. Okay, you're a divorce lawyer. He's a divorce lawyer. Both of you know the path of true love runs straight into the divorce courts. Both of you know love is not eternal. You realise the happy-ever-after-get-married-and-have-kids is a false ending. Or a false start. And yet, here you are, with all the stuff in your life happening to you and your friends, and you talk about him with a gentleness I've never heard you use before. Do you know what, Hazel, this man sounds like a man, not a boy. He sounds like a man. He sounds kind. And funny. And thoughtful. And you've never gone for that kind. You've gone for arrogant, believing it was confidence, selfishness believing it was strength and narrow mindedness believing it was determination. You've usually gone for good looks believing that is what makes good sex. They don't. Some of my best lovers have been pug ugly.'

'Well, I'm lucky there, as he's quite handsome, but thank you for that, Angie. Thank you.'

I get off the couch and hug Angie who is grinning at me. As I walk out the door I turn and thank her again.

'And tell me what he thinks of the arrow, will you? I always like testimonials.'

Next morning in the office, Joe and I are sitting on the desk, kissing. Not like school children. Like adults, knowing what we're doing and why we're doing it. He stops kissing me.

'This is a very grown-up relationship,' he says stroking my cheek.

'Is that a question or a statement?'

'A statement.'

'Just because you're wearing a suit doesn't mean you're a grown-up, Joe.'

'Very funny. You know what I mean.'

''And just because you're going out with someone who is ten years your senior doesn't make it a grown-up relationship. Any way, what is a grown-up relationship?'

'One with no illusions. One with no fairy tale. One based on experience and knowledge and understanding and the reality of what it takes to make a relationship work and how it can go wrong. One where the emotion manages to survive, to seep through, and not blind us, but allow us to see more clearly.'

'You're a poet and you don't know it,' I say, rubbing noses.

'I am indeed. Poetry in motion.'

He lifts me off the table and gently waltzes me round the room, humming something classical. Don't know what. The sunlight is streaming into my slightly untidy office, with its white walls and table and black chairs and obligatory box of tissues and coffeepot and cups. And all I can think is 'this is very gentle and very romantic.'

Joe may be able to read my mind as he says, 'What's your idea of romance?'

'My idea of romance is the unexpected. Originality and simplicity. Cornwall, The Minack Theatre. Crashing waves against a craggy cliff. Tuscan hills in the autumn. Romance is walking along a beach in the winter. Romance is being the only couple on a ride in an amusement park and wanting to go on it again and again and again. Romance is in a restaurant where you can't afford the food but you can the ambience. And you order bread and wine and olives and nothing else. And don't speak for the duration not because you have nothing to say, but that you can't take your eyes off the other person. And you occasionally touch and stroke their hair. Nauseating to watch—I remember watching a couple do it in France over lunch one time—but I knew where they were at. I knew how they felt. Deep down I'm a realistic romantic. That used to make me vulnerable, but it doesn't any more. It makes me stronger.'

'It makes you who you are.'

'I know. My head is in the clouds and my feet are firmly on the ground. It means I get severely stretched as a person.'

'You're quite magical and lovely, Hazel. Do you know that?'

'Brian tells me that every morning when I come through the door. He says "You're magical and lovely, Hazel".'

Joe smiles and kisses me again while we're waltzing and it's lovely. And dancing for a minute at eleven o'clock on a grey Monday morning in an office in central London is now somewhere up there with the crashing waves in Cornwall, Tuscan hills and winter beaches.

Then same day, late in the evening, just out of the shower, hair dripping, about eleven o'clock, I get a text message. It's from Joe.

MESSAGE RECEIVED
Ever had text sex?

First thought, he's been drinking. Second thought, perhaps it's not him so I should check the number. No, the number's his. Third thought, perhaps he feels we've waited long enough and he's as frustrated as I am. After all, it's been a month now, but is that long enough? Is there no mourning period with these men? Slash and burn is obviously de rigeur, but do I want to be a part of it? I keep the answer open.

MESSAGE SENT
You are drunk. Obviously. Go away.

MESSAGE RECEIVED
I'm not. Ever had text sex?

I think this is in bad taste. So say so.

MESSAGE SENT
This is in bad taste. You've just separated from Fiona. Is there no mourning period?

MESSAGE RECEIVED
I'm just asking a simple question. Have you ever had text sex?

I'm weighing up whether I should play this game or not. I think it is a game and not a healthy one, but you never know.

MESSAGE SENT
No, had phone sex though. You need a voice to turn you on. You need to hear the voice. Texting is impersonal. Plus you can get the words wrong.

I know, I tried this with Dominic last year and instead of putting base of spine I kept writing case of prime all over the place. Poor guy thought it was some Victorian term for a part of my body that he had yet to find. He spent hours trying to tease my prime and find that bloody case.

MESSAGE RECEIVED
No you don't need a voice. You've got a sexy voice, Hazel, but I don't need to hear you. First, you ask the woman what she's wearing. Then you ask why she is wearing it. So where are you and what are you wearing?

Where am I and what am I wearing. Right. I'm in the kitchen, just out of the shower, dripping wet with little on. I write...

MESSAGE SENT
I'm in the bedroom. Wearing pink Victoria's Secret, my skin smells of strawberries and not much else. What are you wearing?

I feel like one of those 0800 numbers found in public phone boxes on the Tottenham Court road. The ones with pictures of Jordan look-a-likes. In reality, the women are married, going on fifty, moustached and chain smokers. I know, I represented one of them once and they make a nice little living out of it. Learnt a lot about phone sex from her I did.

MESSAGE RECEIVED
Me all in rubber—is that the sort of thing...

He's obviously in his city suit, too.

MESSAGE SENT
Rubber no good, too difficult to tear off with teeth (let's tease him). I'm wet.

Eek, why did I send that. Bit heavy. He won't answer. I know he won't answer but

BROOOOOMMMMM. The car comes in immediately.

MESSAGE RECEIVED
How wet?

I suddenly don't want to be in the kitchen anymore. I walk upstairs. Well, I run upstairs actually, holding my phone as though it's some sort of lifeline, which at this moment, it sort of is. I make sure Sarah's asleep. Peep in. Yep, she's asleep I think. I go into my bedroom and close the door, put the dimmer lights on mild, so there's a soft half light, filling the room with shadows. I undress, putting the phone down and waiting for the sound of an approaching Formula One car any time. Go to drawer. Find lacy knickers I said I had on. Put them on (this is soo weird). Lie back on bed and think of Joe. In five minutes his image of me is exact. I'm no longer in the kitchen wearing bathrobe (nicked from la Posta Hotel in La Marquee Italy on an exquisite week with Dominic) with wet hair. I'm in the bedroom, with the knickers, thinking of him and sex and sex with him.

MESSAGE SENT
Glistening. Ask me where my hands are?

I'm stroking myself very slowly around my nipples, and down toward my belly button. I admit, I can't foreplay with myself for more than two minutes alas. If I was a man I'd be one of those men women would complain about all the time. You know, 'he just goes for the kill' sort of guys. So my fingers are already reaching into my knickers and stroking, and I'm very wet by the time I receive the next text message.

BROOOOOOM.

MESSAGE RECEIVED
And now very curious, where are her hands?

He's gone into third person. It's somehow safer, as though we're talking about another couple, but know it's us we're talking about. I'm intrigued.

MESSAGE SENT
They are reaching down into her panties. She's gently stroking herself. Where is he?

I hope he writes quick. The fact I have to wait for the sound of a Formula One engine though, makes it more exciting. It's as though I'm playing some sort of sexual Scrabble. If he doesn't get the words right, then it doesn't work, if it does, I go to the next stage. Hopefully, in this game, we both win.

MESSAGE RECEIVED
He is in the bedroom. He is looking at her. He wants to touch her. He can tell she's wet.

MESSAGE SENT
She is.

MESSAGE RECEIVED
Well if she's that wet she may need something dry and hard but not straightaway—perhaps some gentle rubbing first to help with the glistening.

Rubbing, ouch. Perhaps he's not as good with words as I thought.

MESSAGE SENT
Ouch! No way, she's made of flesh and blood not brass, he can sit and watch and ache and be teased while she teases herself just out of his reach. And he can watch as she strokes.

MESSAGE RECEIVED
She may have misunderstood. Rubbing poor word. Stroking touching teasing caressing on his mind. And who

knows he may enjoy being teased. She is after all soft sensitive and glistening. How long he could wait....

MESSAGE SENT
His choice of words is not poor. I'm sure he can be a cunning linguist when he wants to be. Perhaps he should be bold.

MESSAGE RECEIVED
It is true the chance to use his mouth, lips, tongue does please him.

MESSAGE SENT
Where does she want to be touched?

MESSAGE RECEIVED
Somewhere bold.

What the fuck does that mean? No matter, I think I know what that means.

MESSAGE SENT
There is nowhere bold on her body, just soft and smooth and sensitive.

MESSAGE RECEIVED
This girl obviously needs to be touched.

This girl obviously needs to be touched. I reread that line. I like that line. Hazel does like to be touched.

MESSAGE SENT
How does she need to be touched?

MESSAGE RECEIVED
Caressed, stroked.

MESSAGE SENT
If he's not already, she would like him to lie on her bed.
He takes off her panties very slowly. She's asleep. He wants
to wake her and make her moan with pleasure.

A pause. I wait for his next move. Am finding this
quite exciting so don't expect the next message.

MESSAGE RECEIVED
I think you meant to send this to someone else. This is Fran.

I go cold, feel sick. Then laugh. Fuck, have sent the last
message to Fran. The one about the panties. Hey ho,
could have been worse—more graphic. Trust me to send
something to Fran's number instead. I can't even do text
sex properly. I don't want to tell Joe, he might get turned
on by the idea of three in a bed (I expect so) with me
and my best friend (definitely if he's turned on by me),
so perhaps I'll let it lie.

MESSAGE SENT
Wrong person. Aghhh darling now you know how I get my
kicks when I can't get to my man.

MESSAGE RECEIVED
You cheeky minx. Night night Fran x

I'll never live that one down. Something I expect she'll talk about when we next meet up. Please don't Fran. Please don't. But where's Joe?

MESSAGE RECEIVED
He can feel the tension easing in him—surely she can't stay wet for too long? He may not last. Think being blown dry would help his situation. But is she still wet?

I'm starting to get really aroused. I'm imagining Joe on his bed in a similar position. One hand on the mobile, the other pretending to be me. My touch, my mouth, my body. He's watching me play with myself without actually being here. He's in the room. I pretend he's sitting in the corner, under a shadow and watching me intently. He can't touch me but he's watching me and waiting for me to climax. He's listening to my whimpering. But he can't even hear the sound of my voice as I come, but he's there in my mind and I'm in his, so it's somehow more intense. I've decided I need a man who's a poet. Not just good with his tongue, but words as well.

MESSAGE SENT
She couldn't stop herself. She let him watch as she came. Next time, he thought, next time her hands will be my hands.

MESSAGE RECEIVED
Nor could he. Nice end. Sweet dreams. His will be.

I turn off my phone. I will never look at it in quite the same way again.

I wake up wet and feeling horny. This is not surprising since I've been dreaming about sex with Joe all night. Think I was in an Italian villa, taking a shower and he was in the room next door and could hear me taking a shower, and was lying on his bed in a white cotton shirt, which was damp with his sweat. He'd been working in the fields all day or something, though why a divorce lawyer would be working in the heart of Tuscan farmland, don't ask me. It's my dream and I like it. He's lying on the bed and he hears the sound of the shower and he knows it's me taking the shower. This obviously turns him on and he has to investigate. He walks into my bedroom, all ochre stone walls and large wooden furniture tastefully placed. I see him. I'm afraid and excited at the same time but don't cover myself. I'm tanned as though I've been in Italy in the fields myself for a month, and my hair has natural highlights and eyes look white and bright (not the usual bloodshot mess they can look pre–Optrex in the morning). He undresses and walks into the shower. Kissing my neck and turning me round so he can kiss down to the base of my spine, or case of my prime, as Dominic would have it. And then he kisses my cheeks and strokes my thighs, watching the water glide between them. He stands and pushes me gently toward him, kissing me again on the neck and stroking my nipples and reaching down to...

Phone rings. It's Mick. Bad news.

Chapter Twenty-One
Losing Doreen

Instead of going to a wedding at the beginning of August, I am attending a memorial. This is not something I expected. Yesterday Fran, Valerie, Carron and I sat in the middle of Green Park, on a thirty-degree hot sunny summer's day and had a picnic of salmon sandwiches, chicken fillets, olives, fresh figs, dried apricots and dates, Chablis and grapes, just like we always do on Doreen's birthday. Only Doreen isn't there this time. She wasn't there to mark time, or boss us about, or to be late, to tell us how wonderful Jane is, or how well her kids are doing at school, or how sexy her gym instructor is or how Mick is wonderfully endowed. She's not here. There's a dreadful gap. We still laugh and talk about her, sometimes as if she was there, half expecting her to say 'oh shut up talking about me', but she doesn't. She just lets us talk about her with overwhelming affection and indelible sadness.

We promised each other there would be no tears and there weren't. Only tears of laughter at our memories of her exploits. Of her trying to have sex with a ski instructor but getting stuck in her outfit and feeling very frustrated. Of her trying to seduce a famous rock star, but on meeting him realising he was a wrinkled prune rather than a worthy prince. Of her quiet kindnesses, organising for Carron to have an all-expenses-paid romantic weekend away with her new man to Prague, and Valerie to have a £150 a night nanny so she could sleep the first few months of her baby's life.

The picnic scene was set to perfection when I took a photo of us all. All except Doreen. Valerie has brought Nelly who is gurgling at her breast. Carron tells us about her wonderful new man who wants to marry her, but she thinks it's too soon and is on the rebound and doesn't want to go there. And Fran's bump is starting to show. She's very proud of it. She's always been a stick and now she looks like a stick insect that's eaten a ladybird. Although I don't know if stick insects actually eat ladybirds, but you know what I mean.

We talked about how Fran had explained to Daniel that she didn't feel right about getting married and wanted to call if off. And how Daniel had not understood but felt if she wasn't sure it was for the best. And she said it was for the best. He said he only wanted to marry someone who wanted to marry him and knew he was the right one but she obviously didn't. She agreed. Although I think he didn't want her to because he told her that she was no spring chicken and doubtless would be a spinster for the rest of her life. So he's not bitter. At least that's one divorce I won't have to deal with.

Fran explained how she and I had cancelled everything to do with the wedding and explained to everyone about why it was cancelled, and everyone agreed it was the right thing to do. If you're not sure, it was the right thing to do. Fran is such a sensible girl, they said, that she knew it was the right thing. Some claimed she had last-minute nerves, but not many. Most of her friends said that they felt it wasn't right, but never said anything, because it wasn't their place to. So they kept quiet. And I thought isn't it strange how many people keep quiet because they think it's the right thing to do. And sometimes it is and sometimes it isn't.

And they asked me about Joe. How I was getting on with Joe. I said fine. And that I thought I was falling in love with him, because I thought about him a lot, but it was early days yet. And I missed Doreen jibing me about the sex and asking me pointed questions about how big he was and how much energy he had. She was crude but she made me laugh and I wanted to laugh that day. I so desperately wanted her to be there to see Valerie and how she was with Nelly, and how Carron was and how much weight she'd put on since Le Pont, and how Fran was. They all looked glowing and happy and I know Doreen would have been so very happy for all of us. And she couldn't be. She couldn't be happy for all of us because she wasn't there.

The actual memorial service was different. No one laughed. There were over a hundred and fifty people there and everyone cried. Some cried very noisily, others quietly. But they all cried. I spoke and read a poem about a ship passing into the distance. It being like life passing into death, and that death was a continuation of the journey, only that we couldn't see that person any more, but we knew, could sense they were still there. And everyone cried more and mentioned afterward how wonderful my speech was.

And Mick was there. And Jane was there. And Doreen's children were there. Even her gym instructor was there. And they all looked very sad and very ashen and very shocked.

As I listened to others talk about her, I remember going into the hospital with her, and Fran, and sitting down in the waiting room and she was laughing and saying how she didn't like her breasts anyway and she should have had a boob job and that this wouldn't have happened if she had. And how Fran told her about the baby and she said she should have it and that she would support her in anything she did. But that she thought Fran would make a better mother than she would a wife and that most women would and do.

I remember how she went into the surgery, and was there for several hours having a scan and came out grey and unsmiling and said that she had to go to hospital immediately. And that immediately meant later that day.

And that she may only have a few weeks to live. Probably. And that she had so much more to do. So much more to do with her life and she couldn't fit it into two weeks. And that she had an action list like mine, like the one I'd read on the way to EuroDisney, but thought I would find it silly. But that she wanted to bungee jump and learn Spanish and learn to fly. And she didn't want to be stuck in hospital for those two weeks, she wanted to be with her children and Mick and her family and friends.

And I remember how she spent time with all of us in those next two weeks, and we made time for her and returned to EuroDisney and went on all the rides, including Small World, and how she wasn't as well and loud this time, but how she laughed. And she took her kids, and how they laughed. And how she refrained from using the F word.

And how we weren't there when she died, but the last time she saw us all together, when she was a shadow of herself, she said she didn't regret one moment of her life. Not one. And that we shouldn't either. And that she was proud to have known us and will be watching over us—either under our feet or up above, tripping up all our enemies and making sure we were safe and happy and well, and stayed fit and sexually active. And that she would be our guardian angel, for us and our children. And that we must help Mick look after her children and look after Jane. And that everything would be fine. That everything would be fine. And that cancer was horrible, and someone should find a cure for it, don't you think.

Mick told me he was with her when she died. She died at 9:32 a.m. on a Sunday morning, at home, in her bed, and the birds were singing outside and it was due to be a warm day, a very warm day and she was in her Harvey Nicholls nightie and she was in the foetal position. And that she looked so peaceful when she died. He told me he felt her looking down on him when he sat by her side, stroking her cheek. Her cold cheek, but she had looked in so much pain and she seemed very contented and at peace. And that he had cried and that he very rarely cries but that he cried and was pleased the nurses left him alone. And that she had left strict instructions with Jane about what to do, what flowers, where money was to go, who was to be invited, what music was to be played, and what food was to be provided at the reception, who was to read and what was to be read.

He told me in one quiet moment between the two of us at the reception. 'Hazel, I am absolutely desolate without that woman. I'm finding it hard to breathe at the moment. I'm taking each day as it comes. She was so beautiful, in the prime of her life, and such a fighter, she was such a fighter, Hazel. Such a fighter and she couldn't beat this. She couldn't beat this. I'm not a spiritual person but I believe she's still here, with me. She told me she would be. She told me she'd be watching me if I slept with anyone unsuitable after she copped it, as she put it. I laughed of course. But I've spent most of my time crying, and am exhausted, and that's during the night. I've been with the kids during the day, who're very upset but they can't see their daddy upset. They can't see their daddy upset. And, Hazel, I miss her, I miss her.'

Man of millions, ruthless with other men and money, sobs in my arms. He's like a little boy who's lost his mummy. And I hold him tight, very tight, while he trembles with inconsolable pain and stroke his head over and over again, and rest him into my shoulder, into the nape of my neck like I used to with Sarah when she hurt herself at school. And I tell him everything will be all right. Everything will be all right. Everything will be all right.

Chapter Twenty-Two
What Are You Wearing?

I'm fizzing. I've had six Beroccas and it's only just gone ten on a Monday morning and I'm buzzing like a bee on heat—if there is such a thing. I've got to decide what I'm wearing for the New York trip. Okay, it's in a week's time so why am I sweating now? Usually I pack the night before and usually I don't give a fuck. A tight blue suit. A little black dress with jacket for the evening. Anything by Ghost that is squish-up-able, but this time I'm going with Joe. So I'm looking long and hard at my wardrobe. The green Paul Smith skirt and top, very boho chic, and the Franke boots—all from Blue Lawn, best shop in the world in one of the dullest places in the world, Chetley. Yep—but the boots are heavy which means I'll have to take them in hold. Or wear them, but they don't go with the suit. Mind you, I could wear the Paul Smith for the journey. No, it would crease. Then Chine—lacy number and Love Sex Money, which says it all. Knickers all lacy and French and La Perla or Victoria's Secret. I can buy more Secrets out there. Oils, aromatherapy and others for the body. All things Dermalogica. Hair highlighted and trimmed. Underarms, half leg and bikini line waxed—care of Angie.

'So, how are you, Hazel? Did you pull with the arrow. Did Cupid's bow get to anyone?'

'Well, sort of.'

'Someone special or one of your bubblegum men as you call them.'

'No, more substantial than bubblegum.' (Bubblegum men equals men who are sweet and juicy for the first few moments, then just become tasteless and hard work, artificial and wear you down. The only resort is to spit them out or stick them somewhere where no one can see them.)

I tell her about Joe. About Fiona. I tell her that he is bright and handsome, and I think quite romantic, and he works in my office and he's twenty-nine. That we have chemistry and that he's intelligent and sexy and fun. And that we haven't even slept together yet, but we've had text sex. And that we're taking it slowly.

She listens without interruption. She's the only person I know who doesn't interrupt me. When I've finished she tells me I'm right to wait but that will be very difficult and I better make my arrow look good just in case (she's like a little girl, rather sweet actually—getting very excited about the prospect of this man Joe slowing stripping off my underwear and gazing upon her work as though it's a da Vinci). She asks if I feel ready to fall in love again.

'Are you ready to fall in love again, do you think?'

'I would love to fall in love again. I've spent the last seventeen years making sure Sarah is well adjusted and happy in her home. I've focused on creating a little haven for her and for me and it's worked. I have a group of friends who I love and trust and who love and trust me. And I have my health. I've done stuff and have an imagination and drive to do a lot more. Before and after I'm forty. But I've felt for such a long time that I don't need a man. Women don't need men the same way men need women. I've lived by the rule. It's become my mantra. I don't need a man.'

'Perhaps you were too fussy? Perhaps your standards were and are too high?'

'Perhaps,' I reply, 'after the divorce I took a step back and pondered long and hard about what I wanted. I looked at myself and realised that I attracted the sort of men I did because of the person I was. I recently saw photos of myself that David dropped off for Sarah and thought, hey, this is so not me anymore. I'm probably a free spirit, a bit of a control freak and can be quite feisty, so I've tended to attract men who need fire and lack the sense of fun and freedom I have. I've also attracted really arrogant types and because I've come across as quite vulnerable—something I've been told by many men is highly provocative—I've also attracted bullies and men who are insecure themselves. I'm still a free spirit, and have lots of energy, but I'm not vulnerable—or as vulnerable anymore and I don't find arrogance attractive like I used to. I find it boring.'

'So to answer my original question, are you ready for love?'

'I don't know, Angie. There's more to life than love.'

'Is there?'

'Yes, there is. There's children and friends and work and I remember the counsellor telling David and I that we needed more than love to save a marriage.'

'No, you needed more than love to save that particular marriage. And, if you ask me, which you sort of are, that was a stupid thing for your counsellor to say at a stupid time. I've been through it, Hazel, but I still believe, between you and me, love wins over hate and anger and jealousy and fear. That's not just a big screen myth. It does conquer all. Just sounds naff to say it these days.'

'But the men I've loved, love in such a selfish way. They're restless. And if they're not happy they just move on, they don't persevere.'

Angie looks at me, spatula with green gunk in one hand. My legs are splayed as usual and I, as always, find this such a surreal meeting.

'Hazel, from what you've told me about this Joe, he doesn't sound selfish and is anything but a bully. You're the one who is restless. You make them restless. And you allow them to be selfish. They can't be selfish unless you let them. As for your men moving on, they enjoy the thrill of the chase. You enjoy the thrill of being chased. That's natural.'

'I know. But I'm not sure I want to be caught. When I'm caught, all they do is sit on me, eat me and then move onto the next kill.'

Angie applies a strip of wax and rips. Bless her.

'There's a few good ones out there,' she says calmly.

'Mmm, I remember the end scene in that film *Sweet Charity*. The one where Shirley MacLaine played this night club dancer and thought she'd met someone who was noble and handsome and kind and loved her for her, and could be strong enough to deal with her past. He wasn't able to. He let her down. And I remember her sitting in a park in the last scene, in tears, and a hippy came up to her—you know a sixties flower power hippy—and gave her a flower and said, "Love". She looked up and smiled and the credits rolled and the line said *And Charity Lived Hopefully Ever After*. I was only ten when I first watched that film and I didn't really understand it, but I understood that bit, and my heart ached for her, because I knew she was right. That life was like that. And that love was like that. And that all you could ever hope for was hope.'

Angie applies some more green gunk and rips again.

'The best you can do is hope because there is no guarantee in love. And I have always been driven to believe if you want something enough, if you really, really want something enough, you can get it. But love doesn't work like that. It doesn't endure. You see evidence of that every day in your job, Hazel. But perhaps have you ever thought, perhaps you don't want it enough? Not really and now, perhaps you do. Perhaps your subconscious, if not your conscious, is telling you it's time. You're ready and open to it. And you have to be ready and open to it.'

'Do you think I'm honest with myself?'

'Do you?'

'I think I'm brutally honest with myself. Sometimes I daydream, but in general, my work is very much about living in the real world, with real issues, but being aware of how powerful emotion is and the role it can play in making a reality of its own.'

'Your job has probably slowed down the process of being able to accept love, romantic love into your life again.'

'That is an understatement. I hear women, and men, tell me stories about their marriages. And some of them are amazing. You think, why the hell did they last that long? Why are they still together? And they look at you and say "I loved him" or "I loved her" and nothing, absolutely nothing they have said, suggests that they loved this person or that person loved them. And they don't see that.'

'So you believe you're blinded by love?'

'No. I feel perfectly sane before and after I fall in love, but while I'm in love, I'm blinded by emotion. And that's not good because it affects my judgement.'

'You don't see love as a good thing?'

'No, just an inconvenient one. That's bad, isn't it?'

'No, it's good that you realise it. Though it does mean, as you put it, that it will take a very special kind of love to convince you that you should value it as a part of your life.'

Angie rips again. Fuck, this still bloody hurts second time round and it's not supposed to.

'I don't want the pain again. It's the only thing I really remember about my time with David. I forget most things, but that unique feeling of pain. Never goes away. The look on Sarah's face. The claustrophobia of hate in a house which was no longer a home. All these things.'

'But that is the past, Hazel. And Joe is new. And he is a possibility. And he is young. And he sounds different. Give him a chance and listen to him. Listen to what he says.'

'Yes, I know if he says he needs space midafternoon on a Saturday or he is confused, I'll know.'

'You will. You will also know how to behave in such circumstances and to keep your heart open because it's a big heart, Hazel, and it would be a shame to go through life and not experience love again. Do you remember that feeling?'

'Yes, I do.'

'Wasn't it wonderful?'

'Yes, it was.'

'Then hold that thought and fight for it, because it's worth fighting for.'

I see so much fighting between couples who have loved each other. More than that, sworn love to each other till the day they die, and they fight all right. They fight each other tooth and nail for the money, the children, the livelihood, the revenge. I know life is supposed to be ups and downs, but for fuck's sake, why do I get a job where it always seems to end horribly ever after?

Chapter Twenty-Three
New York State of Mind

Brian Stapleton has convinced me that Joe and I ought to have a two-day trip to New York. It is work of course and although no one suspects in the office about Joe and me, I'm sure 'the office knows.' As in, the office knew when Jennifer was pregnant, and the office knew when Brian was having an affair with one of our ex-clients. Rumours seem to spread in the air despite the fact we're all usually very discreet. I've had a call from Jennifer, my right-and-left-arm former PA, who's had a little boy called Horatio Dunstable, which is an atrocious name for such a cute little boy.

'It's an atrocious name, Jenny. Why did you call him that?'

'It's a family thing, Hazel. I don't want to talk about it. He's probably going to be called Horror or Dunce at school if we're not careful. But hey ho, see what happens. How's the new PA working out? How's it working out with Joe Ryan?'

'Marion is fine. Efficient. Not you. Joe is efficient and gets on well with clients.'

'I hear you're seeing him.'

This throws me. Jennifer's good at guessing me, but all I've said is Joe is efficient and good with clients. Is the gossip wind reaching that far these days? How can she guess from those few words?

'How did you hear that?'

'Oh, Brian told me. He says that you're getting on well. That he recognised an immediate spark, but that you've both been discreet and it's rather sweet really, you being so coy about it.'

'So much for our discretion.'

'Whatever. I think he's cool with it.'

'Well, he's so cool with it, we're both going to New York for two days. This afternoon, actually.'

'So you're going out with him?'

'No, well, no. We've had lunches, tea, coffee, drinks. Hugged, we've kissed.'

'It does sound sweet. Sounds as though you like this one.'

'D'you know, Jennifer, I think it is. And I think I do.'

Five o'clock. Same afternoon. Heathrow airport with hand luggage. Possibly one of my favourite places in the world. Edgy, noisy, and if there isn't an air traffic controllers' strike, everyone is full of anticipation, excited in the knowledge it's going to be a long journey. I always think the attitude people have at airports is how people should treat life in general—as some sort of fun journey. They're usually excited about this particular adventure. But most people treat life's journey like a daily commute. They survive it rather than get excited about it. And they take far too much baggage around with them, the physical as well as the emotional stuff. Travel light, I say, and you get further and can go faster. In life and when travelling.

Despite wanting to pack half my wardrobe for this particular trip, I've managed to pack light. It's taken years of practice, but I've perfected the art form. I have hand luggage for two days. Outfit I'm wearing, three pairs of barely there La Perla knickers, two semitransparent blouses, two skirts, one dress, one cocktail dress, small makeup bag. Dermalogica cleanser, toner and moisturiser (the best, in my opinion)—travel size. Would like to take tweezers but I've had five confiscated at airports as potentially dangerous weapons. Brush, travel shampoo and conditioner. That's it. All in hand luggage.

'Is that all you've got? 'Joe asks.

'Yes,' I say. 'Little black dress. Lingerie. Stockings. Extra-strength condoms.'

He smiles.

'No, really. We're out here for a couple of days and I've never seen a woman travel that light.'

'Well, I do.'

I survey Joe's suitcase. It looks as though he's packed

for a two-week ski trip to Whistler rather than a two day business trip to New York.

'Why so much?'

'Oh, I've left lots of space for buying up Timberland stuff. It's so much cheaper out there.'

'Good idea. Why don't you just buy a suitcase out there, too? One of those soft suede ones? They're cheaper there and you can take hand luggage on the way out.'

'Didn't think of that.'

'Well, you'll know for the future.'

'We're flying business class,' he points out.

'The Executive Lounge is nearly empty so we have the choice of seats.'

'Where do you want to go?'

'Oh, anywhere. Not by the toilets, and not too close to the bar and drinks machines. Over there in the corner. That's good.'

I get two diet colas and Joe gets himself a beer and a muffin. He sits beside me. I'm vaguely aware he's staring at me.

'Do you know how difficult this is?' he says.

'How difficult what is?'

'Sitting next to you like this.'

'Well, don't then. Sit somewhere else.'

'It's going to be difficult to keep my hands off you during this trip. To be professional.'

'You want to know how you can?'

'How?'

'Think of Fiona sobbing.'

★ ★ ★

There's plenty of space on the flight, but we're seated next to each other.

'Do you want to discuss our itinerary while we're out there?' Joe asks.

'Yes, fine. I know we hit the ground running. Literally.'

'Yes.'

We pull out our papers and tray tables. The attendant comes round and asks if we want champagne and would we like to order. I survey the menu and order coq au vin and smoked salmon starter. Joe orders lamb with crab starter, with red wine. The attendant hands me a sticker which says DO NOT DISTURB UNDER ANY CIR-CUMSTANCES. Must remember to take this home for my office door. Brian has a habit of just walking in without knocking. As I survey the papers I feel a furtive hand reaching over my thigh and lifting up my skirt.

I like the idea of Joe being so close and yet not being able to do anything. I don't want to join the Mile High Club, but the idea of him sitting next to me, there's very little space between bodies even on business class, for five hours on end is a luxury I haven't enjoyed since I started 'seeing him.'

'How are things with Fiona?'

'It's been difficult. I think she was in denial for a long time, even when we were still living together in the house—and maybe still is. She's angry now, too. She says she loves me. And I love her. But not how, not in the way, she wants me to. And I have moved on emotionally,

Hazel. I realise I've lost my best friend but there's more to a relationship than being just a best friend.'

'That's what a lot of relationships are.'

'When you're in your sixties or seventies or eighties perhaps, Hazel. Not when you are in your twenties, thirties, forties and even fifties. Anyway, she wants to meet up, but it's not a good idea. I've told her this. And she knows I more than like you. And that you're now my girl-friend. So seeing her prolongs the pain.'

I listen to Joe tell me the story. It makes me go cold because I'm reliving the moment when David told me about the other woman, and the words are the same, the phrases are the same, the excuses are the same, only this time I'm not the woman at the bottom of the stairs, I'm the other woman, but I'm one who's got more compassion on her side. More understanding of how Fiona feels and that will help, if I ever meet her again, which, hope-fully I won't. If she turns up at my door again or threat-ens to kill the tortoises, well, I'll cross that bridge, but I'm not wasting sleep over it. I haven't and didn't have sex with him while he was going out or living with her and haven't to date. Well, unless you count text sex, which okay, I sup-pose is sex.

And anyway, I'm his girlfriend. He told me so himself.

So for the rest of the flight, we sit and hold hands and occasionally rub noses and stroke thighs and nothing more. And it's frustrating but just right.

At JFK our chauffeur is holding up a huge placard with RIANNON AND CHAMBERLAINS. Not that difficult a name, but I'm used to it. Even worse when I used my married name. I use to get GROVEL or COW-ARD or best of all BOWEL when I was married to David. Chamberlains and Riannon are driven by an aspiring actor who tells us his life story for the first twenty minutes before he learns that we're divorce lawyers and then sulks for the next twenty when I say his wife will get everything if she finds out about his affair.

We're both staying at the Ritz Carlton overlooking Central Park. I am told J Lo stayed here with Ben and he bought her thousands of white roses and sprinkled the petals all over the room. I'm singularly unimpressed as I know how tiresome it is to tidy up after flowers and the petals rot and the bloody things get everywhere. I like my room, though. I'm in room 1908. Fabulous view of the park. Joe's on the floor below.

'I'm obviously not as important as you, Hazel.'

'Don't think it's got anything to do with it. Do you want this room?'

'No, but perhaps I'll be sleeping in there more than I will my room while I'm here.'

'You know why we've got these rooms, don't you, why we're staying here?'

'No.'

'Brian knows the manager, a former client, who's married well second-time round. Rumour has it that he's also slept with him. But it's only rumour.'

I'm in the bedroom, a bedroom alone with Joe for the first time. Even Housekeeping have turned on the radio by the bed and Billy Joel's 'New York State of Mind' is playing, somewhat appropriately. I suppose it could be worse—it could be Sinatra's 'New York, New York.' I hate Billy Joel's songs normally but today, today I like everything. As I look at my younger man, I know I want to make love to Joe now. In this room, at this moment. I walk up to him and carefully lift his shirt out of his trousers and undo his belt without taking my eyes from his. I think I must have undone every sort of belt known to mankind. Those with buckles, those with poppers, those with Velcro (the men were usually horrible), those with braces (usually city and fat types), and consider myself an expert in much the same way I'm sure men do with bra straps. I don't need to look at what I'm doing—I just feel the way. I slowly undo his trousers. He says nothing, just watches me. I kneel and take him in my mouth. He does nothing for a few minutes, then asks me quietly to stop and lifts me up.

He swings me round and kisses me, very sensually. I feel as though a switch has just gone on inside me, ironically since I also feel as though the lights have just gone out and can only manage now with his help. I realise Joe is pushing me toward the bed, managing to undo my skirt and blouse in a few moves. This makes me think he could have done that a long time ago and was teasing himself by waiting till now as much as he was me. He slowly strips me naked, kisses my neck, between my breasts, moving down my body slowly, slowly to my thighs, remarking on my arrow.

He smiles. 'I haven't seen one like that before. Very exciting.' Thank you, Angie, you were right.

He then reaches up again and lifting himself onto me, pushes himself inside me. He reaches deep into me, exploring me, but he's also exploring me with his fingers, exploring me with his lips, nipping me gently like a cat, stroking me. And I should be uncomfortable and overwhelmed and I'm not. He's allowing me to get to him. To turn him on and things that seem unnatural with other men seem natural with him. Everything is natural and easy and sexy with him. This isn't sex. This is making love. It's the Jane Austen where people got to know each other before they made love, not the *Pretty Woman* contemporary version where people have sex, then get to know each other—if they're lucky. Okay, perhaps not Jane Austen, she would have waited till they got married. And perhaps I should have waited longer. But this is lovely. I can sense he wants to reach deep into me. As deep as he can go. That somehow he wants to get under my skin physically, like a ghost passing through my body and staying there. Possessing me without possessing me.

He stops and looks down at me, stroking my face occasionally and smiling. Saying nothing and smiling. Just kissing me occasionally. After a while, I don't know how long, he says, 'Let's go and see the view.'

Which surprises and confuses me.

We're both naked. He takes me over to the windowsill, pushing me up against the glass.

'Do you think anyone can see you?' he whispers in my ear.

We must be on the 200th floor of this building. I don't think we'll be overlooked. There's one building that's close by. It's higher than ours, but it's not an office building. I can't see anyone there. No binoculars.

He pushes me up against the picture window. Wow, I hope there aren't any birdwatchers in Central Park today. They do tend to have binoculars looking out for the birds. They'd get an eyeful if they fell on this building. But I'm not letting Joe have it all his own way. Let's share the control, shall we? I turn on him and push him up against the glass. Saw this when Ellen Burkin did it to Al Pacino in *Sea of Love* where he thought she was the killer but still slept with her anyway because she was so incredibly sexy, and she wasn't the killer—it was her jealous lover, so bit of a bummer for him. Anyway, Ellen did this to Al and turned him on and, well, seems to be doing the same for Joe.

'The curtains are opening,' Joe says with a start.

'They can't see anything from this distance surely.'

'Can't tell. Could be the maid.'

'Great. I'm pressed up against the glass and there's possibly someone looking at me sprawled in delecto against a window.'

'Can't make out who it is.'

'Does it matter?'

Joe sighs as I'm moving my hands in between his thighs and pushing my body hard against his. I ask him if he's enjoying it. He says yes and tells me he thinks the couple in the other building have binoculars. I say the idea of voyeurs turns me on. That they can't touch us, but they can watch us. But that I don't need an audience to get turned on by him. And with that he draws our curtains and leads me back to the bed.

'We should do some work today.' I say this but don't mean it.

'I know. But we've gained seven hours flying here. Brian always tells us to optimise our time. So let's make good use of a few of them, shall we, Ms Chamberlayne. Then we can get down to briefs.' And he kisses me again and the lights go off.

The work in New York goes without a hitch. The days are spent with our client and the bankers investigating funds that should have been declared and haven't been. Our client can now ask for the matrimonial home because there's enough money to go round, and that's good. It's been successful workwise. The nights are spent in Joe's arms, naked, where time has no meaning and every song about love played on the radio in our room does. You know, the ones that make you normally cringe and want to throw up and think, who the hell would relate to this? And when you've just met someone, or lost someone, you do relate. You so do. And it's been wonderful and just a little unreal. And, I hate myself for saying this, but I think Billy Joel's songs are the best.

Chapter Twenty-Four
Bad News

Back in the London office, humming a happy lyric to myself, Joe comes up to me.

'Got some news. Not good. Can you come into the meeting room?'

'Of course.'

I follow him in, thinking, I know, we've just slept together and he's decided now he's getting back with Fiona. That's it.

Door closes.

'Mr Benson just called me. His wife has tried to commit suicide.'

I'm shocked. I'm so shocked I burst into tears. I'm shocked because I've burst into tears. I don't burst into tears. It's not that I'm hard but stuff like this happens sometimes with clients. It just gets too much for them.

All this hate and stress. But it doesn't get too much for me. This is my job and I don't burst into tears in the office. Ever. Joe looks surprised, but hugs me.

'Hazel, what's this now? This has happened before with clients. Occasionally. One goes off the rails, loses hope, doesn't get enough professional support, or emotional support from family and friends. This happens. Why this woman?'

'Oh, I've had one hell of a roller-coaster three months, haven't I? I've lost one of my dearest friends to cancer, one of my other friends is now not getting married, something she's wanted all her life and is having someone else's baby. I'm losing my daughter and best friend to college. And I've met you, and any moment now or tomorrow or the day after tomorrow, you'll be poised to turn round and say "Hey, I've made a mistake. I've decided to go back with Fiona." After all, that's what I was hoping with David all those years ago, that he would just turn up at my door and say he'd been wrong. And I know you're different from David and Dominic and even Benson. I think you are different. I think you do learn through experience—your own and other peoples'. And I've just started to believe in the idea of happy ever after, even after separation. I know it sounds so naff, but I've started to open my heart to the idea of love, to tentatively being in love again and someone's just gone in and stamped all over it.

'Things like this happen. You can't judge all relationships by this one.'

I brush my tears away with tissue from the box usually designated for sobbing clients. I feel a bit stupid. I feel very vulnerable.

'It's good to hope for happy ever after, Hazel.'

'They are for fairy tales. I can't believe them, Joe. I wouldn't be able to do my job any more. I'll be telling clients that love conquers all. And to go back and pore over the original love letters they sent each other and look at their kids and ask them to fight for it. Fight for the relationship because it's worth it. Instead, what do I do? I rub my hands, add up my hours and invoice them for £300 an hour excluding VAT for their pain and my time. This job is an internal discipline for my heart. We strip the emotional away from a situation which is highly charged and see the wood for the trees. That is what we do. We tell people what they are entitled to, not what they deserve which is a subjective, altogether more emotive area. That is what I do. And I do it well. I've done it well. And perhaps, I can't do it anymore. Perhaps I see a moral dilemma when I think, hey, I'm making money out of someone else's misery. What's the value in that?'

'The value in that is that if we weren't involved it would be far messier and far more miserable than if we were. Good divorce lawyers do their job, explain the situation to the client and calm the situation down. They lay the material facts out. The counsellors deal with the emotional side. We are not counsellors.'

'I know that. Perhaps we need to be. Have more empathy.'

'Hazel, you know as well as I do, if we had more em-pathy, we wouldn't take on half the clients we do, because we would have a big sign up on our door saying NO WANKERS ALLOWED. That would seriously cut into our client base. Don't you think?'

'Yes. I'm just going through a phase. An "I'm in love" phase and I'm…'

I've said it. I've said it. I've told Joe I'm in love. I haven't said I'm in love with you, but I've said I'm in love, which can't leave much to his imagination. And he thinks I'm silly now because I've only known him several months and I feel I'm behaving like a child. It's like calling my-self Hazel Ryan in a Freudian slip, which you only do when it's on your mind. And this is ridiculous. And I'm furious with myself. I haven't been this vulnerable for years. Please God let him ignore that. He heard.

'And I'm in love, too. And it's wonderful and special, like the woman I'm in love with. And I'm going to hold on to it and work at it, and see it for what it is.'

I didn't expect that. I didn't expect that response. I've got so used to cool, calm, collected responses from men, I didn't expect I love you, too. I haven't met or perhaps, if I'm honest with myself—haven't encouraged a man to be so open, one who is so collected at work, but who I've made into, well, a loved up boy. For so many years I've thought about the men I've met and thought about how they've treated me. And how I've treated them. I would ask my father, who died over seventeen years ago now of cancer, what he thought of them. I would ask in my head silently to myself what he thought of them. There was always a no that came back. Sometimes I felt I could even hear his distinct laughter and see him shake his head at me. A whispered no which echoed through my mind, that I didn't even tell Angie or Fran or Brian or even Sarah about. And now with Joe, I ask him again and I don't get a no from my father's whisper. I get a maybe. I get a maybe and a smile.

I can feel myself falling. I can feel myself wanting to believe Sweet Charity finds a love somewhere in Central Park and lives happily, not just hopefully, ever after.

Chapter Twenty-Five
Hazel Makes a Decision

Angie drops her wax.

'What an awful time you've had, Hazel. All this has happened. Bloody hell, girl.'

I've told her about the wedding that was called off, about Fran's baby and about Doreen.

'I didn't tell you last time, Angie, because, well, I was still in a state of shock and you were asking me about Joe and stuff and if I was ready to fall in love and I didn't want to burst into tears. But it had to happen. And it happened in the office, in front of Joe, when I heard about someone trying to commit suicide. It just triggered the tears.'

'Well, stuff always happens together, doesn't it. And it's good to cry.'

'And Sarah's going off to college. I'm losing my little girl.'

'You'll have plenty to do and she will be in contact for money if nothing else.'

'Sarah's very independent, she'll try to deal with things by herself if she can.'

'She will, but she'll be in contact. How's work?'

I think about work. Work is fine. Brian has been very sweet and kept me busy and given me a larger office to make slightly untidy. I've kept him informed of every-thing and he's allowed me to take time off, but thinks work is best, and working harder is best still. Which I agree with. Although it's avoiding the tears that's toughest.

'Have you cried much?'

'Yes, loads. In private and in front of Joe.'

'And has he been supportive?'

'Very. Very supportive. But I don't want to depend on him too much. I've fallen in love with him, Angie. I've allowed myself to fall in love with him and I've made my-self too vulnerable. I feel as though I need to be needed and need company and need love and need to be cud-dled and nurtured a bit. And there's nothing quite as bor-ing as someone who's needy, especially a woman.'

'I don't think so. Sometimes when you allow your guard down, Hazel, it's the way people can get to know you and it seems that Joe wants to get to know you. You come across as independent, but I don't think you're as independent as you appear. You've been thrust into the situation. By your divorce, your lifestyle, the fact you have a busy life and you can manage your own finances and have had to do this by yourself. But I don't think you're independent, Hazel. You're a little girl, too, sometimes, but you know you can't be. Now Sarah's flying the nest, you don't have to be a mother anymore, not a day-to-day one anyway. You can be a child again if you want to be. Do you want to be?'

'I don't want to be a child again, Angie. I'd like to have some fun. I'd like to do some of the stuff on my action list. I'd like that villa in Tuscany, learn that language, write that book.'

'What's stopping you?'

'I am.'

'Have you discussed this with Joe?'

'Yes, he says I should go for it.'

'How is it going with him?'

'Very well. I still have that will he, won't he feeling about Fiona sometimes, but he's been so straight with me all along, I think that's over for good.'

'Is he serious?'

'Serious in the fact he says he loves me. Yes, he's told me that. We enjoy each other's company to the extent we don't have to talk, we just sit in restaurants and look at each other and don't have to say a word. Nauseating to look at I'm sure, but wonderful to be a part of.'

'Have you heard from his ex again?'

'No, not since she appeared at my doorstep that time when I was with the girls.'

I think back to the time, when Doreen was still alive and laughing with us about her boob job and I start to cry. Angie hugs me for a long time. Stroking my back and saying nothing. Just listening to my sobs. After a while, she pulls me away.

'See, you do need mothering occasionally.'

'Yes,' I blubber.

'Have you met Joe's mum?'

'Yes, I've met his mum and dad. They're lovely. Absolutely perfect.'

'So everything is perfect.'

'Yes, everything is perfect, then why aren't I happy, Angie?'

'Because you've lost a best friend and it's made you think what is important to you and that time is precious and you have to live for the now and you want it, whatever it is, to start now, and everyone's life is taking a new turn—Valerie's, Carron's and Fran's and yours is as it was before Doreen died. Yours is constant and you feel you should change but you don't want to because, horror of all horrors, I think you're happy. And maybe you've never really been happy until now. Scary, isn't it?'

'Something always goes wrong when I say I'm happy, Angie.'

'With pleasure there is always pain,' she says as she starts to wield the green wax and rip again, which is slightly less painful than before but only slightly less.

I return to my office, sore between my legs and probably looking sore round the eyes. I find Joe waiting for me in my slightly untidy, slightly larger office. He looks white with nerves.

First thought—oh fuck. I knew it. I just knew it. I had to admit I was happy out loud to Angie, didn't I? And hey presto, life fucks me right back and goes aha. Fooled ya. Let's screw up your happy ever after, girl. And now, Joe is telling me, he is telling me he's going to go back with his ex. I just knew it. And bugger, I've run out of tissues. Take it on the chin, Hazel. Just smile and listen and sit down.

He kneels at my feet.

'I want to know if you would do me the honour of being my wife?'

He is on bended knee in my office at two on a Tuesday afternoon, looking up at me expectantly. This is very odd. I don't expect this. It's not as unromantic as first time round, when David proposed in Waitrose over the scallops, but it's unexpected. I'm a romantic and midweek afternoon in my office is stretching it a bit, even if it's the thought that counts—not enough thought has been put into it for me. I say nothing.

'I know this must come as a bit of a surprise, but I've been thinking about this for a long time. I've been thinking about it since the first time I met you. And realising how precious time is. And when your friend died, I realised just how important time is, and Sarah's nearly gone and I want to show I'm committed to you and to our relationship and I love you, Hazel Chamberlayne. So will you do me the honour of being my wife?'

I am still lost for words which is unlike me. I, too, realise Doreen's death has made me think differently about spending time and not wasting it and living it to the full. Though do I want to live it as a Mrs again or is this me time? My time as a single woman, with Sarah at college and being a support to my friends but also delivering some of my action list. And if I became a wife again, would I be able to do all this? I love Joe, or think I do, but am I at a different life stage to him and does that matter? I seem to want the same things he does, have the same values, the same ideas. I hadn't thought until now that the ten years mattered but he wants marriage and I don't know if I do. Not now. I want to learn new stuff and not go over old ground, because that's the way I see it. Marriage, children, mothering and seeing them grow and love and learn and leave. And do I want to do that all over again. Live that life all over again. It wasn't a bad life first time round, despite David's foibles and controlling bullying ways. And Joe's much, so much better. Not the bully David was and probably still is. Do I want the same pattern again for the next twenty years, albeit learning from the last twenty or do I want to follow a different path, a more selfish one, one that expands me in a different way, that doesn't involve children and marriage and husband? Or is that what life is all about and not just a social control to keep us in place and in fear and in love and on side. Hey, what the hell do I know?

So I smile at Joe and say, 'No.'

Pause.

'I've been there, Joe. I've been married and had children and I want to live a different life, not another twenty

years of the same. I know I love you. That's what I know.
I just don't want to live by the same rules, the same con-
fines as I did first time round. I've learnt those lessons and
I want to learn new ones. I want to broaden my horizons,
perhaps buy my place in Tuscany and live there some of
the year. I would love you to share that with me, but I
want to live by my terms and share my life with those I
love. I realise I don't want to do *this* any more. This going
to court and dealing with people like Mr Benson over and
over again. It's not doing me any good. I can still see the
joy in the sunshine on Monday mornings, but how long
for? How long will I be able to see sunshine when there
is none? I want a different view, not because I'm restless,
but because I want a different view now. A new challenge
while I still have the health and energy and enthusiasm
to do it with a full heart and bank balance. And I want
to experience all those things that Doreen can't and I've
hopefully got more than two weeks. Do you understand?'

Joe looks at me as though he doesn't, as though I've
broken his heart or his pride or both. He stands up, glazed-
eyed, says nothing, turns and goes, closing my door quietly behind him.

I stand there looking at the closed door.

Knock. 'Can I come in?'

Brian's voice and face appears, beaming.

'Is it congratulations then?'

'No,' I say. 'I said no.'

He looks shocked. 'But I…'

'I know, Brian. I've said no because I don't want to get

married again, not because I don't love Joe. I do. I love him and understand what love is all about. I think I'm at a different stage in my life to him and don't want what he wants, which is understandable and is perhaps the barrier to loving and being loved by a younger man. I've already learnt the importance of love and friendship and most important of all, being a mother and it's wonderful, but perhaps I'm the Peter Pan now. Perhaps I'm the one who wants to learn to fly and wants his freedom after all. Would you be dreadfully upset if I resigned, Brian?'

'Hell, Hazel, you know how to surprise a man. First, saying no to Joe, then offering your resignation. Have you had one of those visions or something?'

'No, not at all. Okay, Doreen's death had something to do with it. It made me think about what else I want to do in life. I want to share it with Joe, if he will let me, but I want to do it on my own terms, not anyone else's and I can't do it working here day in day out.'

'Can't you just take a sabbatical?'

'I don't know if I'm coming back.'

'Does anyone? I would rather live in hope that you're coming back than close the door completely. It's never completely closed, Hazel.'

'You'd do that?'

'Yes, I would. I would do that.'

I smile and hug Brian.

He gives me a kiss on both cheeks and tells me Jennifer called after me and asks if she can bring in Horatio to see me and I say fine. As he leaves he says, 'And you're silly saying no to Joe. He's a good egg is Joe. He may be young but he's got a wise head on his shoulders.'

'If he loves me, he will let me go.'

Brian smiles. 'I think differently. How about, if he loves you, he may not.'

Chapter Twenty-Six
The Italian Job

I am no longer a partner at Chamberlayne, Stapleton and Ryan. I've resigned but Brian says he will consider it a sabbatical and if I don't return, he'll look for someone else. He says there will never be another me. And demands I keep in touch. I say I will. I don't have a mortgage but I am looking for a villa in La Marquee, one of the prettiest regions of Italy, as yet undiscovered by *BBC Holiday* programme or *Daily Telegraph* travel writers. I'm looking for a house for no more than £100,000 that requires little renovation, has some land and a view and three bedrooms and a large kitchen and friendly, preferably Italian neighbours, whose families have lived and worked there for ages and would love a beautiful forty-something woman living amongst them, for six months of the year at least.

I had thought about buying in Florida. Not Orlando, because although I love Mickey Mouse, I'm not that enamoured with theme parks. Not Naples, because it put me off when I drove there and the first thing I saw was a cemetery, albeit a well-tended one. I wasn't interested in Spain or Portugal (too many English) Cyprus or Turkey (too far and too hot), and although France was almost there—Italy won over because I love the chaos and the way the people are about life, (they are never black and white about anything) and though I would never marry an Italian (I'd get too fat) I love the idea of flirting with them. Plus, I love their country.

Sarah supports my idea to buy a holiday home, as do the girls who all want to visit and help out. But Fran is now seven months pregnant, Valerie is still breastfeeding Nelly and Carron, bless her, is thinking about marrying this man, who I've yet to meet but sounds wonderful in and out of bed. I miss Doreen dreadfully. A gap that makes me wake up at four in the morning crying, feeling empty. That sort of miss. I miss her energy and aggression and fire and wish she was here to see me pursue something else on my action list. Like the fact I'm learning French and Italian now and getting on rather well. I've booked my next skiing holiday, a diving instructor's course and riding lessons, the first one of which I've already taken. The erotic fiction will have to wait as I'm not being inspired at the moment, not having a man in my life. Instead, I'm writing a diary about my adventure, hopefully turning it into a bestseller that will make me a fortune, so I can buy another, larger place in Italy, perhaps Siena or Rome or Milan. I don't know. These are dreams but I can make them real. I know that now.

I look at three different properties, each within my budget which Henri Chattani, local garlic-smelling rotten-toothed estate agent has shown me. All have views, all require no renovation, and all I want to buy. One has an olive grove that reminds me of the time when Joe said he would take me to Verona and make love to me in an olive grove and never did. And probably never will. So I'm torn about choosing that one. The memory is both wonderful and sad. I love olives but perhaps it will bring back painful memories, but I can't always think about olive groves that way. So I choose that one. I check out the land, complete the papers. I don't hear from Joe. I know he's still working at the partnership because I speak to Brian and speak to Jennifer and keep Angie updated with all my progress and Mick as well, who may be coming out with the girls later on, with or without Jane of whom he confides he is 'very fond'. I wonder if that was the affair Doreen suspected, but I say nothing. Not the time or place.

I ache and yearn for Joe, but I'm sure it will pass. It's like a shadow hanging over me that I may have made a mistake when he asked me to marry him. I want to be with him though I don't want to marry. And he's obviously hurt. He may have even returned to Fiona who would love to marry him and have his babies. It's done now. And can't be undone.

I miss Joe's sense of humour. His dry wit. His energy. His love of life. I thought I'd just miss his smell, the sensuality of us making love, as we did in New York, but it's more than that. We waited or seemed to wait an eternity to get it together and it's made the bond stronger between us and I keep thinking I've made the wrong move. By saying 'no.'

I tell Fran one night, on the mobile, while sitting in my new home, drinking a bottle of Chianti.

'Have you called him?'

'No. I think I hurt him and, well, saying no to someone who proposes, and that was a big thing for him, he's probably back with Fiona now—with ring and wedding arrangements no doubt.'

'Do you think so?'

'I don't know. Brian says he's doing well at the partnership and has lots of women after him, but he doesn't seem to have anyone serious at the moment.'

'Do you regret saying no to him?'

I lie.

'No, it was the right decision for me at this moment in time. I'm not ready to get married again, not in a conventional means anyway. Perhaps to a bohemian man who loves to paint and can earn and still make me laugh? Perhaps then I can be with someone, but I don't want a husband, I just want a partner, a companion, a lover. I'm more interested in quality of life now than stuff. My first forty years were full of getting stuff, accumulation of stuff, stuff I needed and stuff I didn't. And getting power.

Power I needed and power I didn't. And now, I've got everything I want in a material sense and just want my friends around me, to be chilled and happy and—'

'And write your book.'

'Yep, may write the book, but everything's been quite straightforward. Thought it would be more difficult than this. Even learning the language has fallen into place. Everyone's been friendly and, well, it's been good, as though it was meant to be.'

'It was.'

'I think so, too.'

'Anything missing.'

'As I said, I miss Joe. I miss his cuddles and kissing and conversation and texting and phone calls and his smell and touch.'

'And lovemaking?'

'That's part of it, not all of it. I also miss the closeness.'

'Do you miss Sarah?'

'I get her on the phone every day, Fran. She misses me more than she thought. She still needs her mummy.'

'We all need our mummy, Hazel.'

'I know.' (I think about how my parents would have loved the house.) 'You're coming and then Valerie with Harry and Nelly and Carron with her man, and Brian says he's flying over on business and will pop in probably with Jennifer. So it's going to be a full house this autumn. Autumn in Tuscany. Perhaps I'll call my book that.'

'Too naff. Probably one out there already.'

'Okay, okay, it's early days. I haven't written first word yet.'

Fran, aware as ever that I miss him despite my attempts to digress, changes the subject back to Joe.

'But you'd like to see Joe?'

'Of course I would.'

'Why haven't you called him?'

'Because he would have called me, if he wanted to speak to me.'

'Perhaps he thinks you would have called him, if you wanted to speak to him. Plus, you're not prepared to admit you may have been wrong. Call him to find out if he's still hurt.'

'You think that's a good idea?'

'No harm in trying.'

I click off to Fran and click on to Joe.

Four rings and no answer. It will go onto answer machine soon.

'Hello.'

I wait, thinking it's the voice mail.

'Hello, Joe Ryan speaking.'

It's not.

'Hello, it's Hazel. How are you?'

Silence then, 'I'm fine. Good to hear from you. Hear you've settled into a villa in Tuscany. How is everything?'

'Fine. Good. It's beautiful here.'

'I'm sure it is. Chancery Lane looks pretty cute today as well.'

'I'm sure it does.'

Silence again.

'How are you?' I ask again.

I want to say so much more. I want to tell him I miss him and I love him and I've been thinking about him every second of every moment of every day, and that it's wonderful here and I would love him to come and visit and bring Sheila and Norman because they would love it. And I want to tell him I want to go to Verona, take him to Verona and make love in the olive grove and possibly even in my one. But I don't. I just ask how he is for a third time.

'How are you?'

'I'm fine,' he repeats.

I wonder if he wants to say a lot more, too. If he wants to say that he still loves me and wants me and thinks about me and wants me lying next to him and stroking him and gently kissing him, like he used to. And if he still wishes he had followed me and pursued me. I wonder. I wonder if he's grown younger in his outlook and I've matured. I wonder if we could meet in the middle somewhere. If we could both lose some pride and reach each other.

'I might be coming over to Italy in a few weeks. One of the clients is Italian, and I've got to fly into Rome.'

'Why don't you pop in?'

It's about six hours' drive from Rome, but he doesn't know that.

'Hazel, it's about six hours' drive from Rome.'

'How did you know that?'

'I looked into it, Hazel. I thought about visiting you but it's too far. And, well, I can't go that extra mile.'

'No, I appreciate that.' (We both realise we're talking about something else completely.) 'Well, thank you for thinking about it anyway.' (I want to change the subject.) 'How are your mum and dad?'

'Very well, thank you. They ask after you. They thought you were lovely. I told them I proposed and told them what happened. They thought I should follow my instinct.'

'You obviously didn't.'

'I have started to trust it more, perhaps I'm growing up.'

'Perhaps.'

'Anyway, I understand why you said no. You don't want to feel tied down again. You've done the marriage and having children and divorce thing and don't want to do that again. I understand that. I don't want to clip your wings. I would never do that. But I know myself and I do want to get married, Hazel. I want the fairy tale that most women want but I want it with a woman who doesn't. That's the irony.'

'Perhaps you want it because she doesn't.'

'No, I like the idea of spending my time with you. I like that idea.'

'You don't have to be married to do that, you know. You don't have to have the certificate to secure my commitment. As you know, the certificate is only a contract should anything go wrong. A backup clause, something to protect both correspondents. It makes sense, but I don't want that now, because I know how I feel and God knows how I feel, and you know how I feel and that's enough for me. Those who bear witness in the church, those friends and family, invariably lose contact or let you down. You don't need to get married.'

'How about children?'

'How about them?'

'There's still that stigma of children being born out of wedlock.'

'Like most things that will change over time. Like most things it may take longer but it will change.' (I pause and take a breath.) 'Look, I'm not saying I won't get married, I'm just saying not now. I want my time; me time, but I'd like to share it with you, on my terms.'

'So no compromises?'

'Not if the compromise means getting married and coming back to the UK. No. That's not compromising, that's giving in. And I don't do that anymore.'

He pauses, then says, 'Strange it's the man who wants the fairy tale and not the woman.'

It's funny listening to a man saying that phrase, 'I want the fairy tale.' I don't want that anymore. I did when I was in my twenties and thirties. But ultimately I was trapped and limited by a fairy tale that wasn't my idea of ideal. But not now. I want to live life to the full, to live the dream, to make it a reality. A part of my reality, which is now in La Marquee, I've made real for myself. And Joe can choose to be a part of it if he wants to. But the fairy tale, that particular one, I don't want anymore. Actually, I'm not sure I ever did.

'Take care and God bless, Joe.'

'You too, Hazel.'

I put the phone down, feeling so very sad and empty, as though I've drunk too much coffee and nothing else for days. I feel stronger because I've explained myself, and if Joe wants to be with me, he'll find a way. I want him to prove himself to me by accepting me on my terms. Just for once. This once. And if not, well, shit happens.

To be honest, I'm desperately wanting him to read my mind and translate me like Fran does. I don't think that film with Mel Gibson got it right. Women aren't that simple. Relationships aren't that simple. They're complex. That was how men thought women thought, not how women actually think, which I don't think would make a good film. Or not a film that would be understandable. Or translatable to a male audience, anyway.

But I'd like Joe to translate me like Fran does. Probably because Fran would listen to me and tell me I love Joe and want him here. That I want him to share the dream I've realised, I've tick boxed, which I know he would love. But hey, I wanted to say more and didn't. Yes, I know what I've done is best for me, what I think is best for me, and know that if it's meant to be with Joe, it will happen. And everything happens for a reason. And perhaps I'll meet someone else. A handsome Italian stallion. And I don't want to put pressure on Joe. I want him to make the choice. Of his own free will. I want him to want me enough. To really, really want me enough to get on a plane and be there for me, with me. And at the moment, he doesn't, but that's okay.

I sit in my porch trying to type the first pages of my book, which I'm thinking of calling *How to Handle Hazel,* and dedicating to Sarah and the memory of Doreen. I'm having writer's block. I can't work out how the hero handles Hazel, because despite having forty years of being me, being Hazel, I admit that I'm still not sure how to do it myself. I know I'm happy with me, just need to find someone who is as well. Or put myself in a position where they find me. Whatever. I'm too busy living to worry. I think a mixture of passion and kindness and humour mixed in with compassion might go down well, but perhaps not. My life doesn't seem to be black and white these days. Plans go awry and all my friends are not where they thought they would be a year ago—even those who had planned every last detail, including Fran and Doreen. Perhaps you have to get to forty to realise it's useless to plan. You just need guidelines, and being happy with yourself is the most important guideline you can define. I'm cool with that. My life is not grey, it's a different hue. A different, brighter, unexpected colour.

I've brought about thirty books with me, many of them Booker Prize and Orange Prize book winners that I bought at Gatwick Airport to distract me for the few months I'm here. My book may not be as good as any of them, but I don't care. I'm going to make it happen. It's going to be a work of fiction, based on a woman finding life and love in the Italian countryside. Okay, okay, I know it's been done before, but mine's going to be different, sassier, sexier and more three-dimensional. There will probably be a divorce in it somewhere, and maybe some phone sex, but we'll see. Only page one so far. So with laptop turned on I look out over the olive grove in my garden, my beautiful garden, losing myself in the warmth and the smell of fresh basil that I've just picked for the mozzarella and tomato salad I'm having later.

I sleep restlessly that night, but early in the morning, about six o'clock, I'm woken by a noise outside the house. Perhaps Fiona has sought me out in Tuscany. I wouldn't blame her, although I did allow him time and space to think. As much as you can when you work with someone.

I open the door and see Joe standing there, looking rather dishevelled but smiling softly at me. I want to cry. But I don't.

He walks toward me and strokes my hair and says, 'I thought I could give you some ideas to start your book.'

'So you got on a plane.'

'Yes, always best to communicate face-to-face, don't you think?'

'Yes,' I say.

'What do you think of this?'

He picks me up in his arms and walks me to the bedroom, occasionally kissing me and talking as he does so.

'Hot Italian countryside. Our hero, still sweating from another day debating the sort of case that would make the hardest of QCs weep, takes a break. Walking into his bare but charming room, he struggles to take his shirt off, still wet from the day in court—beads of perspiration clinging to his back. Lying on his bed, the cool white sheets give a moment's pleasure till his heat dampens them. The shutters are open, and he can hear a shower start in the room next door.'

He lays me on the bed and starts to undress me.

'It's her, but did he imagine it? Yes, he asked her over to look at the paperwork, yes, it was a masterpiece of appraisal but how she did gasp, and linger by his side, and maybe for a moment it felt like she was breathing him in. Yes, his smell was a mixture of sweat, aftershave and heat—but hers, well, hers was like sex, a powerful mix of tropical forest, the warmth you feel on a hot beach and that perfect delicious smell of, well, of her. He then realised his descriptions were...'

And starts to stroke me, very slowly up and down my body.

'Crap.'

I giggle. He continues to stroke and talk.

'But that didn't matter. She's in the shower, water running through her hair, down her back, what he would give to...'

He leans over to kiss me between the legs.

'It had been too long. Our hero, exhausted by the heat and the sound of flowing water could bear it no longer.'

He slowly undoes his shirt and leans over me again.

'He must find out if she wanted him. Perhaps when their hands touched on the dance floor, in the office, over the coffee it was a mistake. He enters her room, she's still in the shower, is facing him now, naked but not shy—he wants her. She is stunning.

'Where's your shower?' he asks matter-of-factly.

'Over there.' I smile.

He leads me toward the bathroom, turning the water on roughly so that it spurts out cold everywhere, making us laugh.

'It's supposed to gently trickle. Gently trickle, not cascade frigid water. It's supposed to gently trickle down her body, her hands guiding its flow between her legs.'

We stand. His arms are around me, he's watching me and watching the water as it gradually warms and I enter, taking the soap and doing as he says.

'He is lost in her. No longer able to control himself. But fully aware of why he's doing what he is, he can't resist her any more. He wants her. He needs her. To be with her. And then she realises. And admits. That she needs him, too.

'How does that sound?' he asks, joining me in the shower, kissing me very gently on my closing eyelids and then on my cheeks and on my lips.

'Wouldn't happen in real life,' I say. 'Wouldn't happen in real life.'

FOR BETTER OR FOR WORSE?

Everyone tells Sarah Giles how lucky she is to be with Paul O'Brian – a handsome city hot-shot who's steady, financially secure and knows how to throw the perfect dinner party. But her seemingly blissful relationship has been celibate for nearly five years.

Sarah isn't looking to be rescued. But what began as an innocent office flirtation is fast turning into erotic obsession. Sarah's plunging deeper into a double life. But which life is the lie?

www.mirabooks.co.uk

MIRA

THE FIRST YEAR OF THE REST OF HER LIFE?

A tipsy confession of infidelity during their engagement hadn't been the best start to Sarah's marriage. It had taken Paul O'Brian five years to propose, and even then he'd made only occasional guest appearances in Sarah's bed.

Now, five years and one child later, Paul had decided it was time to cut their losses. Determined not to go under without a fight, Sarah is catapulted into an unforgettable last year of being married.

www.mirabooks.co.uk